I0818588

The DIARY of a LUTYENS' PRINCESS

The DIARY of a LUTYENS' PRINCESS

BINDU DALMIA

RUPA

Published by
Rupa Publications India Pvt. Ltd 2016
7/16, Ansari Road, Daryaganj
New Delhi 110002

Sales Centres:
Allahabad Bengaluru Chennai
Hyderabad Jaipur Kathmandu
Kolkata Mumbai

Copyright © Bindu Dalmia 2016

This is a work of fiction. Names, characters, places and incidents are either the product of the author's imagination or are used fictitiously and any resemblance to any actual person, living or dead, events or locales is entirely coincidental.

All rights reserved.
No part of this publication may be reproduced, transmitted, or stored in a retrieval system, in any form or by any means, electronic, mechanical, photocopying, recording or otherwise, without the prior permission of the publisher.

ISBN: 978-81-291-4039-5

First impression 2016

10 9 8 7 6 5 4 3 2 1

The moral right of the author has been asserted.

This book is sold subject to the condition that it shall not, by way of trade or otherwise, be lent, resold, hired out, or otherwise circulated, without the publisher's prior consent, in any form of binding or cover other than that in which it is published.

To every woman who retained her arrogance in never bending her head before the insolent might of man or destiny... She is my heroine, the ultimate princess of my book.

For she is Shakti, the force which holds and nourishes this creation. It is from her that all emerges and into her that all dissolves.

Is she you? For she is me...the complete me.

Contents

Preface

IN YESTERYEARS, PEOPLE would pen their innermost thoughts in a diary and hide it, hoping no one would ever lay their hands on their secrets. Diaries were personal recordings of triumphs and failures set against a certain zeitgeist and our consequential reactions to those goings-on in the socio-political world. A cumulative of what then became recordings of collective history.

All beings are products of their times and their emotions are their subjective reactions to those ambient occurrences. Etchings in a diary do run the risk of sometimes turning into self-obsessed narcissistic renderings, a flaw I was conscious of refraining from. If anything, I tried to depict the truth in its nudity: naked and bare, with no place to hide.

I then compiled these writings in the nature of a deep prayer, an ode to those that impacted my life and shared the 'Pilgrim's Progress'.

Humans are the sum total of their inner world, manifested in outer reality, in a state of constant reaction to our outer occurrences, towards the prevailing rulers of the day and the sentiment of the times. The politics of the day then becomes the first draft of what can be construed as the history of a bygone era.

This is in complete contrast to contemporary times when everyone puts their innermost thoughts on social media, a new-age diary; every family picture goes on Facebook, every thought goes on Twitter. People write before thinking, then regret and delete! My scribbles in my diary were no different, except that they rolled out as stream-of-consciousness thoughts that I wrote as they flowed.

~

LSR: Literate Social Responsibility

I pledge that all proceeds of this book will go towards the upliftment of underprivileged women and accrue to the Prime Minister's Fund towards a deserving cause. Whether the earnings are meagre or a fortune, writers and artists seldom depend on a livelihood from the luxury of their craft. Let's let go of royalty from a book or a biography towards empowering someone's life. No one chose the poverty they were born into. Because poverty is a prison in this lifetime, 'a prison without bars'.

Princesses don't just live in cities. It's a distant dream for a village belle who tills her land with tears…sometimes her wages getting depleted with funding her husband's country liquor. She, to my mind, is a true princess at heart, yearning with woebegone eyes for a life she dreams of, but will never probably see in her lifetime. I want to empower her, whether it's by owning a sewing machine, arts and crafts, computer literacy, or whatever her calling. It may be a trickle, but every drop contributes towards cosmic consciousness. Big corporates are mandated to contribute to the government a small percentage of earnings by way of CSR (corporate social responsibility). If in creating art we can afford to relinquish our earnings voluntarily, let's make that our contribution: LSR, literate social responsibility. Nothing would be more gratifying than to know and feel that one's work lived on for a larger purpose.

We, the privileged, have been blessed. I implore any author, should they write 'fiction-with-a-conscience' to set a noble trend to let go of the proceeds of art towards the Prime Minister's allocation towards where we can use a God-given skill to revert towards Creation.

Unlike contributing towards causes where accounts may possibly be opaque, we do know that this channel of funding through the PM will reach direct beneficiaries and bring a smile to their face, lighting up their lives.

And how inspiring is it for any artist to see that beautiful visage of a smiling woman? A muse in itself to write more, sculpt more…

> *'A person breaks down completely when he becomes dependent on others. In such a situation, he would think of dying, instead of living such life. There is no better thing than bringing such persons out from that miserable situation.'*
>
> —Hon'ble Prime Minister
> Narendra Modi

Part I

'Youth is wasted on the young!'

Baalikaa Vadhu

Calcutta, 1967

> *'Love asked, whispering, "Once you said that you would cherish your grief forever? But have you now changed?"*
> *I blushed and said, "Yes, but years have passed...and I do forget."*
> *Had her tears then learnt the language of smiles?*
> *That's when Fate intervened and spoke thus, "What was sorrow once has now become peace."'*
>
> —Rabindranath Tagore, *Jiban Smriti*

I WAS ALL of thirteen when I met my first love, adamant to nest with him for the rest of my life. Stubbornly wanting to defy my orthodox parents, I couldn't wait for my eighteenth birthday to get married, being a rebel without a cause during my adolescence years.

Arnaab and I first met at a 'jam session' in Mocambo. It was the equivalent of today's play dates, a school social at a restaurant, my first outing with boys when we had no exposure to co-education nor did we socialize with the opposite sex. I was sitting with a group of friends, all of us at that giggly silly schoolgoing age, when none were trained in etiquette or possessed conversational skills, when a stranger from the adjoining table came across in an attempt to strike up a conversation with me, 'If I asked you for a dance, would you refuse?'

'Yes I would,' I snubbed.

'I said "if I asked you to dance". I never actually asked you to dance, ha ha!' I felt slighted. Wasn't that a breach of etiquette, considering he didn't even know me to half-proposition me in this weird way? I came home and vented my anger on my elder sister, who always used me as a guinea pig to try out her latest cosmetics. That day Aradhanaa brushed on bizarre mauve eye make-up on my lids and got me to tint my hair a deep mahogany. I was already feeling uncomfortable and out of my depth to step out to a school social but it was too late to do anything to change that look. Red-faced on my return after Arnaab's half-proposition, I came home and sulked with my sister, 'Didi, how could you do this to me!

'Do what, Aksh?!'

'It's all thanks to the way you dressed me today that no one asked me to dance. Please keep your beauty advice to yourself in the future, Aradhanaa.'

'But baby, why this tantrum?'

'Didi, all my friends were hotties with no make-up, but they reeked of their moms' "Intimate Cologne". When I asked to borrow yours, you and mummy said little girls don't wear fragrance. My friends knew how to do the twist and waltz too. When one guy from La Martiniere asked me to waltz, I was like Zorba the Greek, stamping his toes. You are elder to me, why did you make a monkey of me?'

To be older and wiser, as they say, you have to have passed the route of being stupid and young at some stage of life.

Arnaab was not a fabled knight in shining armour but an

intelligent, humble, humorous and affable being, hailing from middle-class origins from Calcutta like my own parents, my dad being a senior bureaucrat in the finance department with the government. Those were years of scarcity, with paltry material possessions and limited means, yet infinite power and stately bungalows were conferred upon government officials.

Arnaab was then a struggling executive with Hindustan Lever (now Hindustan Unilever), while I was an average student in Loreto Convent with nuns as my mentors. Mother Teresa's city, the 'City of Joy' as it came to be known, had a very egalitarian, socialist ethos in the 1970s. The affluent were few and far between, the plebs and upper middle class outnumbered the rich, while the creamy layer comprised of zamindars, the cultural-literati elite, corporates and officers from the services.

Calcutta of 1967, the years we were teenagers, was a period when an activist, idealistic youth were moved to revolution by the poverty they saw in the villages of Bengal. Landless tribal peasants in the village of Naxalbari rose in revolt, organized by Bengal's communist cadres into combative civil strife, as farmers attacked and killed zamindars, redistributed hoarded grain, ransacked homes and set up guerrilla people's courts to mete out a justice of revenge. Students marched with placards of Mao, painted blood-red slogans on walls, organized peasants for long marches and participated in killings of landlords, moneylenders, businessmen and attacking the establishment.

Against the backdrop of this movement, in contrast to the strife of the Naxals and dire poverty of the masses, twenty years post Independence, relics of the British Raj were still all-pervasive. A certain privileged lifestyle was evinced amongst the bourgeois brown sahibs, as they were called, who prided themselves, despite being less affluent, as being more refined than the landed zamindars when it came to etiquette or finesse. Then there were the highly cultured intellectuals who were futuristic thought-leaders, believing 'What Bengal thinks today, India thinks tomorrow'. In hindsight, as Bengal's regressionist economic policies played out, the state remained stuck in a time-warp, leaving that aphorism a wishful dream even after sixty-eight years of freedom.

The colonial hangover was in evidence in British-built country clubs, with portraits of Queen Elizabeth gracing the entrances of the Bengal, Calcutta and Tollygunj clubs, while some, like the Boat Club, were out of bounds for the dhoti-pyjama-clad Indian gentry. Dress codes stipulated a suit and tie, whilst children rode ponies on pristine turfs surrounded by acres of velveteen grass, accompanied by nannies and fed on a staple of fried fish and chips, very Anglo-Indian club fare. This was a world completely cordoned off from the squalor of hutments built with sackcloth amidst ghettos of poverty, in contrast to the pipe-smoking sahibs, served their 'chota-pegs' by liveried waiters, frequenting cabaret shows at Golden Slipper, feasting on turkey and Dundee cakes on Christmas Eve. Park Street, the heartland of Calcutta, came alive with trees, glittering stars, angels and children streaming in to sing carols in merriment as New Year and Christmas were the high point of annual revelry.

My childhood was rooted in the joie de vivre of this culture; Dad and his elite bureaucratic circle being counted as the Punjabi suited-booted, teetotaller sahibs, while Mom was entrenched in the literary world of reading, playing bridge and being a practising lawyer.

Sundays were days to punt a hundred rupees, or if you were in the big league, a thousand rupees, at the race course. That's what the oldies did as a leisurely pastime over weekends.

The comely ladies of Calcutta, adorned in chiffon sarees and coiffured chignons, accompanied their brown sahib suited-booted husbands to the fashion soiree, daintily sipping the young twining tea leaves of fresh Darjeeling Lopchu in the shade of the club lawns. A bit reminiscent of the image one would conjure of lords and ladies parading at the hamlet of Ascot's equestrian extravaganza viewed by the British high-browed, adorned in their oversized, motley feather hats and hand gloves that hid perfectly manicured fingers under them. Except that the ladies' hands at the Calcutta turf were not as neatly manicured as the Duchess of Ascot's, as grooming was rather nascent in India then.

Feigning knowledge about the horse and its pedigree, and even the adeptness and weight of the jockey, these veterans roamed around the Turf Club with binoculars around their necks, chatting up trainers to acquaint themselves about the fitness of the horses that were to run that weekend before they placed their bets with their weekly savings.

We, the school- and college-going teenagers, hung out on Sunday afternoons at Mocambo, or if it was packed, you could squeeze a place with your date on the dance floor to jive or twist at Trinca's or Firpo's. Living on paltry pocket money, we tried not to order anything, but if we had to, then a Coke costing two rupees was enough to be entitled to a dance with the afternoon beau. As the crooner cooed 'Strangers in the night', locked in embrace with a school love, it felt like it was a moment in eternity... Dumb love? Innocent love!? Puppy love? Jam sessions were frequented in the afternoons on Sundays, quite an un-amorous hour indeed by any standard, to be the perfect time to profess love or arouse any inclination of romance.

However, there was a known caveat unspoken amongst us all: before Mom and Dad returned home from their races at

Calcutta Turf Club by 6 p.m., we had to seem like we were home before they returned, appearing to be immersed with 'mugging' (a colloquial synonym those days for cramming and grappling with our homework). We were not allowed to meet boys and even a whiff of a clandestine visit to the jam session was enough to incur mom's wrath and be gated from any further wayward outings for the next week. A very disturbing dilemma indeed. A mortifying thought for a fragile young mind!

To be candid, neither our parents nor the nuns really educated us about the birds and the bees—sex, boys, puberty and menstruation being taboo topics in that era. It was in a science class, maybe in class 5 or 6, that it was very clinically taught to us. You had to make sense of science and translate its emotional meaning as a 'do-it-yourself' exercise in what conjugation could possibly mean in an adult world. Nobody taught you about love or sex, till you stumbled upon the facts yourself and grew up by sheer instinct.

∾

The nuns who groomed us in academics, etiquette and morality were strict foster mothers. But by 2014, a disparate view of them had emerged, in the Age of Modi. They were vilified as perpetrators of conversions, demon-like creatures who were out to 'wipe out Hinduism from the land of its birth'.

In all earnestness, this was not my experience of being under their tutelage in a convent. I saw no evidence of attempts to proselytize young impressionable students or deracinate us from our Hindu roots. Loreto Convent was a Western institution and other than reciting at daily mass 'Our father who art in heaven-hallowed be thy name...' visiting the chapel within the compound or Christmas celebrations, these benign nuns did nothing as severe as impose their religion on students who came from diverse faiths. Hindi and Sanskrit were very much part of the curricula as in any other school run by the government.

Scholars, historians and the intellectual elite who dominated public discourse in 2014 had begun a severe condemnation of Western cultures and values. Right-wing nationalists and left-wing Lohiaites along with Gandhian socialists wanted to stem the tide of Western culture that they feared was out to sabotage India. The Indian Renaissance of 2014 implied a rebirth of socio-cultural awakening to undo historic injustices, quite forgetting that we live in an interconnected universe where evolution is the result of millennia of exchange between cultures, and that no country ever grew in isolation.

This left my generation as nowhere men and women. Having studied in a post-colonial world and imbibed the tenets of a free world culture, we were suddenly being asked to shed our Western influences and speak, write and think Hindi and Hindutva. This was an identity crisis for my generation in our fifties. We, the hybrids, were a confused lot by 2014, guilty of not knowing our heritage and culture adequately, considered semi-pariahs amidst this new revivalism of Indianness.

❧

My father was a bigoted, stern, no-nonsense man. His daughters were not allowed to mingle with the opposite sex, as all men were 'rascals'. *Pride and Prejudice* or *The Age of (No) Reason* summed up his stance. Whatever the hurdles, I learnt at a young age to be on the right side of authority and yet have my way. A rebel at heart, I was constrained to subscribing to conformity in order to adhere to an austere father's rigid code of morality.

The men his daughters would marry were mandated to

be good, virtuous Punjabis, preferably from the services, who had no vices like smoking or drinking, and if this basic bio-data was not met, the girls dared not step out of the Laxman Rekha he drew. Dad's dictates and fatwas were reminiscent of a medieval, austere, khap-like morality, similar to what is still prevalent in the hinterland of Haryana, where marriageable girls had to surrender to conservative authority of antiquated elders demanding subservience to an archaic culture of male dominance.

In short, my dad's preferred choices for his daughters were bores, as he opined that they made for stable spouses and would not turn out to be philanderers. Actually so boring that no other woman would even want to strike up a chat with the lad (forget tying a lifelong bond in wedlock with the twit). The truth was that my cousins from Amritsar found their matches through matrimonial advertisements in *The Times of India*. A rare breed, so motley, you could turn suicidal just looking at their moustaches. I had visions, nightmares, of seeing myself wedded to one of this species, sitting behind them on their motorcycles, where the high point of my life would be a picnic at Victoria Memorial wearing a bilious green salwar kameez and yellow ribbons in my plaited hair, eating jhal muri, the height of a cordon bleu experience. 'Eeks! Dad's choice… those motley men in their flying machines,' I confessed to a friend.

'Daddy, Daddy, Daddy! How could you have got it so wrong, Dadoo?' Daddy Cool had no inkling that his daughters' mindsets were not like those of girls mentored in guru-kul patshalas, but like those exposed to a near-Western culture. Under his austere auspices were two daughters who aspired to marry men who were club-going, knew how to waltz, jive and twist, had wit and humour, and could at least take them to Kashmir's Lake Palace for their honeymoon. London was an idealistic, far-fetched dream only the super-rich went to for their getaway.

Dad was transferred to Bombay soon after I had finished my schooling in Calcutta. Saddened beyond words, I felt this would be the end of Arnaab and my dating. We had begun to meet every day after my school ended. Should he write letters, my snoopy parents would read them, and if he'd trunk call, we couldn't have talked freely. It traumatized me so much that just so I could meet Arnaab once a month, I decided to study in Lady Shri Ram College (LSR) to complete my graduation. If nothing else, I would at least be able to write a letter a day in the privacy of my dormitory, except that I hadn't envisaged the hardships of life in a hostel with stinky loos, or having to make my own bed, or the bullying that I would be subjected to by seniors... All for love, just so that I could receive Arnaab's trunk calls at an ordained time, waiting near the call booth at the corridor, or get to see him a bit more, away from the vigilant eyes of my parents. Arnaab also saved diligently from his stipend as an intern in Hindustan Lever just so he could come by train to visit me as often as his finances permitted over the weekend. I wrote to him nearly every single day for those three years.

~

The mid-1970s

LSR was a fun academy, coeds being unheard of those days. I wasn't brilliant at my studies or good-looking. In fact I was closer to being a simple plain Jane who nurtured no false illusions about my appearance. But I loved the faculty and the friends I made, gradually getting used to the discomforts of hostel life, but loving the little bit of independence that boarders enjoyed.

Ragging was a ritual and those initial few weeks of bullying were a strange leveller that seniors put one through, though over the years I heard it had gotten worse and become a form of sadism. Scared, shy and a loner, I was reluctant to parade for the annual beauty contest the freshers had to participate in. I hid in a friend's room, lacking the confidence to walk the ramp or answer the weird questions contestants were teased with. Some sneaks managed to find me in my hiding spot. So I went through the drill in a simple cotton saree with no make-up, and slapped on a pair of earrings. Clumsily, I walked onto the stage, made a U and turned around. The judges first made me pick up a kerchief dropped on the floor, as they gauged poise by observing how daintily one bent to pick up a fallen object. This wasn't anywhere close to being a glitzy sophisticated pageant like those today. I was relieved the preliminary round had ended and I could coil into my shell. The three semi-finalists were then made to walk the ramp a second time. 'Akshraa Khanna, please appear for the final round, wherever you are.' I had locked myself in the toilet when Vanisha, my best friend who knew where I was, came to get me out. Red-faced, I was up for scanning by the judges a second time in the semi-final round, in which I never imagined I would be included. 'So Akshraa, when you finish college, what do you aspire to?' went question number one.

'Ma'am, I am sixteen years old and the dreams I chase change by the day. At a personal level, I hope to marry a kind man who will fill my world with love. At a professional level, my ambition is to work my way up to someday becoming the CEO of a company.' The panel of three looked approvingly and nodded, leaving me underwhelmed about how my reply had been perceived.

Question 2: 'What makes you blush?'

Answer: 'A compliment, as it rarely comes my way.' Thunderous applause ensued. I had said something spontaneous but silly, it seemed. They laughed outrageously. I was choking within with tears knowing I had said something stupid yet honest.

'What is a philosophy that you hold dearest in your life?'

'To retain my values of being kind, compassionate and non-violent to man or animal, and to never knowingly cause pain or bring tears to anyone.'

'Okay, in this rapid-fire last round, if you had a choice to impersonate three people, who would those be and why?'

'Uh, that needs some thought. Give me a moment to jog my mind please… Okay, I would pick Indira Gandhi, because she's a steely-willed and powerful woman. Mother Teresa, because she's noble and benevolent. And Meena Kumari, the actress, because I see a sadness in her personal life that she's able to reflect in her acting. Oh, may I add one more please? Jackie Kennedy Onassis, because she had the conviction to love again.' A louder applause came my way. I think they liked it. Or were they amused again? Twenty minutes later, I was crowned Ms LSR. 'We are pleased to announce the winner of this year's contest is Akshraa Khanna.'

I was pink with disbelief and embarrassment at the proclamation. This time I had to walk solo for another round, to be crowned with honours. Tears streamed down my cheeks. It was too good to be true: Ms LSR! I thought I was dreaming; or had the judges been mistaken to have crowned an ugly duckling? Was this a cruel joke, me being a beauty queen? Was I hallucinating? Half-compliments I was used to being conferred in condescending terms till now were that I was 'sweet', 'cute', 'fair-complexioned', I was 'loving'…but never ever did anyone tell me I was 'beautiful', not even my own parents or Arnaab, both who loved me dearly.

∾

Arnaab was thrilled and proud of me when I informed him. But when Daddy heard about it, he was unimpressed and even a trifle angry. 'Akshraa rani, you were sent to study and make something of your life. How could you ever participate in a contest for beauty! Had you won an award for your brains, we would have applauded you. Kindly use your time productively. Beautiful girls eventually become models or filmstars. Our conservative society thinks little of them...' Dad rambled on. All I know is by the end of his lecture, I felt more like a sinner than a beauty queen!

Three years flew past while I studied in LSR College as a boarder and dated Arnaab as he settled into a secure job with Hindustan Lever. I trunk-called Mama one day and said, 'Please Mom. Now that college is ending, I don't want to come home. I want to spend the rest of my life with Arnaab. Will you both please consent to this and give us your blessings?'

Dad wrote me a stiff letter.

> Akshraa, if you want to defy my command and marry a man who is not from our community, you stand dispossessed from my estate. Know that in my family children speak very little to elders and you have the audacity to present a fait accompli to your parents! Besides, he is a dark-complexioned lad, I hear, unlike our goraa Punjabis... If this is your choice, you will never be welcome at home ever again.

Arnaab's parents were small-town folk who worked in the steel town of Jamshedpur, extremely lovable in their simplicity. They expressed their intent to call on my parents to ask for my hand in marrying their only son, simply because they believed they wanted to support their son's wishes, not interfering with his choice of free will in selecting whoever he wanted to settle down with. My parents grudgingly agreed to meet them, only to display, by their reserve, a snooty contempt for Arnaab's family because they were Bengalis. Mr and Mrs Chatterjee brought a simple box of sandesh as an offering for my parents, which Mom accepted condescendingly. While the elders talked, I took Arnaab outside to the small balcony outside my bedroom that faced the Hoogly River to watch the boats stream by. We chatted for a while, oblivious to what was transpiring in the drawing room between the elders. I was to learn later that while we were outside, my dad's elder brother took over the conversation and told Arnaab's parents, 'You see, Mr Chatterjee, Akshraa has just finished her BA. She must go on for higher studies as she is too young to marry. How much money may we offer your family so that you stop pursuing our child? It's just a small token, so please don't misunderstand...we could even help Arnaab get a promotion, or find him a better job. He seems to be a fine lad and we do believe you deserve a good Bengali bahu, someone within your own community.' It hurt. It hurt really, really badly when I came to hear the truth of what had happened. My family elders had got my back up by putting forward a crass monetary proposition to Arnaab's parents. It was my first brush with materialistic adults who felt money could buy anything. The incident disturbed me deeply, but humiliated his parents beyond words. Mr Chatterjee felt small and he abruptly commanded his wife Shibori and Arnaab, 'We must leave now. We have overstayed their hospitality. Sorry, Mr and Mrs Khanna, if we took up your valuable time. We loved this little girl Akshraa so much that we only came to offer a formal proposal, as the children seemed so attached to each other. We have not come to sell our son, nor ask for your favours, or eye your wealth and status. Arnaab is a hardworking and well-educated boy and he needs no patronage from a powerful family such as yours… We take your leave. Namashkaar.'

I saw them leave. After that I did not want to stay a minute more in my parents' home. I rushed to the balcony, crying inconsolably, watching them leaving. Being eighteen and financially dependent, I had no choice but to stay. I went into my room, hugged Noddy, my dog, and locked my room from within to mark my protest. By then I had developed a sly and stubborn resolve to oppose my family and stand by Arnaab. The day I turned eighteen I was all set to get married, come what may. But ultimately, Mom's tender heart yielded, not wanting to forsake her daughter on the biggest day of her life. She defied Daddy's writ, taking a stand in coming to bless the wedding and performing the kanyadaan. Dad rigidly stuck to his guns and refused to come to terms with what he perceived as a betrayal by his most loved child. It didn't end there, as that led to a conflict between my parents for some years, something I held myself acutely guilty of for many years down the line.

On our return from our honeymoon in Kashmir, Ma and Baba, Arnaab's parents, organized a big reception in Jamshedpur, as they weren't going to forsake their only son. In those two days I glimpsed their modest lifestyle in a government home and sweated it out without air conditioning. I thought to myself, if that was a sample of life ahead, what now?

I was forbidden from entering my parents' home for nearly eight years after we married. The first few years went by blissfully. Arnaab offered me a life as sheltered as when I was living with my parents, just with lesser comfort. Way back then, I was obedient and unspoilt. Our needs were modest and we both worked in earnest to afford ourselves a decent standard of living.

The guilt of disobeying Dad, however, started gnawing so deeply at me that I turned moody, petulant and offhandish in my behaviour towards him, often temperamental, never giving him the best of myself. After the initial years, there was nothing but tension at home because every little fault of Arnaab was exaggerated in my mind. My elder sibling had married a rich older man and lived in a prime address that had an ocean view, a building which was home to leading industrialists. We lived in a tiny flat. Our richer friends served Scotch and we served Indian Black Dog. How infra! They had big parties, while we struggled to entertain at a club. They owned wardrobes that overflowed from end to end in their cupboards, while I rotated my ten sarees, three pairs of earrings and two pairs of heels. The disparity between my sibling's lifestyle and ours was huge.

I made life a living hell for no fault of Arnaab's. He wanted out. He was done with my shenanigans. I could do nothing to retrieve or set it right ever again.

In the midst of this, I gave birth to my most prized possession, a bonny boy Vishal, who was to be my toy, companion and soulmate for life.

A love story that began in school ended in heartbreak within the first few years.

ೋ

Arnaab and I managed to revive our bonhomie after a mildly acrimonious period post our divorce. As it was a mutually agreed one, corking champagne the day it formally ended was an unusual closure, done so in a spirit of congeniality, not rancour.

Somewhere, we both concurred that teenage loving was cute, but to decide on whom to spend the rest of your life, at an age where neither was exposed to the outside world, was a blunder. We made allowances for each other's naiveté, so we never really lost touch for many years thereafter.

~

Marry in haste, repent at leisure and restart the charade of life a second time!

I packed my frugal belongings, worth a paltry ₹35,000 that I had earned as a model, to migrate to the big bad world of New Delhi, like a refugee in search of her destiny. I was a small-town damsel venturing into the capital's capitalist big world of vultures (or opportunity), with no clue where destiny was leading me.

Relocating from 'The City of Joy' to the City of Power

1983

UNLIKE AN ASPIRING starlet arriving in Bollywood in search of fame and fortune, I was in search of a livelihood so I could stand on my feet. Delhi was rugged and rough in every way.

Making friends amongst the charmed circle and gaining acceptance or inclusion into the Lutyens' creamy circle felt intimidating at the outset.

I was young and demure, fairly aware of a modicum of charm that I possessed, but used it sparingly to get by in the world of the rich and powerful. I had arrived in the City of Power. Power never slept at night, nor did power intrigues or power play. If you didn't match up in looks, lifestyle, pedigree or performance, you were extinct. All four parameters were vital in one's social curriculum vitae. One had to be shrewd enough to not fall into the clutches of a predator in search of prey. The rules of the game were savage. Hell, there were no rules! It was the rule of the jungle, urban troglodytes on the prowl, like brutish cavemen in search of a victim!

I had travelled by Rajdhani with my son, arriving with a modest black trunk that contained everything I owned in the world in the twenty-seven years of my life, my sacred Gita being my most valuable heirloom. After reaching the railway station, Vishal and I sat on my trunk waiting for my maasi, who was a bit late in picking me up, amidst the tyrannical heat of the Delhi summer.

We reached her bungalow in Defence Colony and she lovingly escorted us to her plush guest room, which was to be my temporary abode in transit till I found a job and an affordable room in the vicinity. 'Maasi, I've unpacked. I think my belongings are so lightweight and frugal, like a fakir's, but my emotional baggage is heavier than my luggage.'

It took three weeks of temporary shelter before I found a two-roomed barsati apartment. The vastness of Delhi re-endorsed my feeling of being a small fish in a big ocean, a speck in the cosmos of the capital of India. The terra firma below, the azure sky above, and my paltry belongings would have made anyone feel like a bewildered orphan. My helplessness made me cling to my six-year-old Vishal, who was more worried about the friends he had left behind, with occasional queries as to when his father would come to call on us. The feeling of being in a new city, with a new life and new acquaintances, was more frightening than exhilarating.

My aunt and uncle were a very sociable couple who had a large circle of friends and were so outgoing that I seldom saw them sit at home. A first-generation rich entrepreneur, Maasi had grown to create a mini-empire, a fashion house of international repute. She was my confidante, a fairy godmother I could tell all to, without a fear of her tattling my darkest secrets to my parents. The only piece of advice she gave to me was, 'Now Akshraa, this is the first time in your life that you will be living in an apartment alone. Never misuse your independence and the freedom of being single. Be classy and live classy. Chose the company you mix with discerningly, as Delhi is full of "floozies" who can lure you. And lastly, never indulge in licentious conduct that will reflect badly on your family or have ramifications on Vishal's life. These are the rules I set for you as your guardian. Other than that, you have my word that nothing you share with me will get to your mom or dad. Deal?'

'Obviously, Maasi, that's a given. Point well taken,' I said as I pecked her on the cheek. Delhi's social circuit in the 1980s was as xenophobic to outsiders as it remains today, unlike Calcutta where the social divide was not so exclusivist. The contrast was particularly glaring and hit hard as I was exposed to an elitism I had never known, a motley mix of heady power, politics and old money versus the nouveau riche. Barring my three-year stint in LSR, where boarders were allowed out of the hostel only once a week for a night out at one's guardians' house, I had no experience of socializing here as an adult, since I had gone back to Calcutta and settled into married life with Arnaab.

It was a fragrant summer night in the capital, where the aroma of motia-scented air drowned out the whiff of colognes that emanated off elegantly draped women in chiffons and men in white starched kurtas at a party Maasi hosted. Amongst my initial encounters was a self-anointed Earl (of Nowhere), a sardar from Jalandhar whose real name was Eashwar Singh. The Earl had a French beard and a mischievous smile, with his hair in a ponytail that made him appear a wee bit artsy. His wit was captivating. He was the fabled rake, a man on every mom's 'forbidden-to-meet' list, the kind of guy women pursued like a fatal attraction because of his charismatic humour and showering of fake compliments. He cast a sinister web around women who loved a chase. The more he ill-treated or dumped them, the higher he went in the eyes of his poker-playing cronies, who weren't as lucky as him to attract nubile and young hopefuls.

There exists a type of woman who is enamoured by a bad boy simply because he's elusive and seemingly unattainable. It satisfies a sense of perversity, a need for momentary conquest, if she got to enjoy a few outings with the Earl. He had this distinctive Punjabi-English accent, flaunting his limos and a home with a Jacuzzi, very rare in the '80s. Rakes also come in different forms, some sophisticated, some crass. I was told the downside to dating this uncle-friend of my maasi was that he was the kiss-and-tell type, who regaled his cronies over a game of poker in the afternoons with his stints the night before. Those poor old men were left panting for more of his verbal porn. I swear I saw many aunties eager to catch his attention in the 1980s, though I never fathomed why. He was always attired in safari suits, almost like a uniform, the in-thing for men to possess in their wardrobe in the last century.

When I came across him two decades later, the poor surdi had shed his pomp, slightly bent and bald with age, though his dress style of safari suits remained the same, except that his suit now smelt of mothballs from a distance. Not much had changed in his repeating the same jokes, but he now sounded more like a fuddy-duddy uncle hanging around the Gymkhana Club bar with other fossils like himself, desperately trying to make himself sound relevant to appeal to a new crop of younger friends.

The gentry I encountered at Delhi's gatherings struck me as a far cry from the sophistry of Calcutta. The likes of the Earl at Maasi's party were in sharp contrast to the 'brown-saabs' of the City of Joy, who were a genteel, rarefied and pedigreed breed of aristocracy. Their demeanour was distinguished, their dress sense immaculate. They wore black ties to sit-down dinners; were cultured; never spoke money, though flushed in wealth; spoke the queen's English with modulated cadences, as they rolled their 'Rrrrrs'; and never ever talked sex, a taboo topic in their Victorian correctness, forget bragging about who you slept with the night before.

Now, at one of my aunt's parties, the Earl had begun to cast his seductive prowess over me, a newcomer to the city and a likely candidate for his flirtatious advances. 'You are Indira's niece, I was told? Allow me to introduce myself, I am Earl Singh. I've lived in Delhi for years, an old-timer you can say...' The other uncles and aunties present seemed a trifle formidable. At least he was friendly and charming in a warped way.

Demurely, I put my hand forward to acknowledge his introduction. 'Pleasure to meet you, Mr Singh. I notice this is a very close-knit circle here, so you all must be friends for a long time.'

'You've got beautiful hands, lady. No, actually, all of you is beautiful...not just your hands. Wonder where Indira's been hiding her pretty young niece all these years!'

I wasn't immune to his compliment, but he seemed like a wannabe I could handle with the arrogance of youth on my side. How did I care if he was rich or (in-)famous?

But I cannot deny that he definitely had a presence.

'I notice from your opening line that you have a fetish for hands, Earl Uncle?' I smiled coquettishly, looking into his eyes a moment longer than a glance warranted for a first introduction. He was old enough to be called 'uncle', but charming enough to drop the deference to his age. 'I am Akshraa from Calcutta and I just shifted to your city two weeks back. I am looking for a job and searching for a place close to Maasi's house so that I can feel the comfort of proximity with family in a new city.' I reckoned he had heard that I was recently divorced, as he was known to do his homework before zeroing in on his fancies.

'Sweetie, I am extremely well connected here to help you with both, a good job and a residence. Do let me know if I can be of use in any way. Being new around here, you probably don't know too many people. I guess you will take a while to find your groove but trust me, once you do, you'll never miss Calcutta.' Even if I had misread his innuendo, mistaking his earnestness to help as sounding faintly patronizing, I knew he had taken an instant shine to me.

'Akshraa, you come as a whiff of fresh air in the sultry summer of this city. Allow me to felicitate your arrival by hosting a small sit-down dinner in your honour for just, say, twenty-four people? You will meet some of the whos-who of this city, coz that's how many people the dining table by my pool can accommodate. Would you be gracious to accept my invite and give me a day when you are free?' He hinted he had connections but didn't really drop names, in all fairness.

'Thanks Earl, but I haven't been introduced to your wife yet, so how can I accept your hospitality? Is your better half, the Countess, here at the party? Could you point her out to me, please?'

'Akshraa, my marriage ended some years back, so I don't possess a countess to introduce you to! That place is vacant in my life. I think I am happier being a bachelor.' He grinned. 'Maybe someone as lovely as you could someday step into her stilettoes...'

I wasn't so vain or stupid as to think this was a proposal, just a subtle manner of warming up to me. He persisted with nailing me down to a day and a date, 'So do give me a day and time for me to plan an evening around you?'

'Earl, thank you so much for the indulgence. Can we do so after ten days, as I am preoccupied with my son leaving for his boarding school? He's off to Sanawar as his holidays end soon, so I want to spend all my time with him till he goes. I am going to miss him a lot. Does that work for you?' I replied.

I was aware I was playing hard to get. Should the Earl have fancied I was predisposed to him, I was playing his game. A guessing game. But games only last for a while.

I played the little-girl act, coy and enjoying his attention for the evening, but I was not stupid enough to take a passing fancy home and dwell over a flirt-by-night uncle.

Hmm! An induction to the smooth operators of the capital. Nice. I was getting a feel of the city...

❧

Then there was Sulochana Mehra, a dusky, dominating, slim and slimy, richie-rich, bridge-playing friend of my maasi. A bully who would intimidate, shout and scream if she was losing on the card table, yell at the staff if her tea was not strong enough, throw a tantrum at the hostess if her home was not well air-conditioned, anything to let off steam as she was a bad loser. She was by nature a habitual opponent, not necessarily because she disagreed with you but because she acquired stature by diminishing someone else's. She was now an affluent cougar, widowed a few years back, her coal magnate husband having left her a fortune to splurge on for the rest of her life.

Sulochana had time and money on her hands in her seventies but few to share it with, as her erstwhile friends shunned her cynicism and sarcasm. Cougar she was because she splurged her cash on toy boys for company, not really for sex as she had passed her prime, since only money could buy her friends in her ageing years. She never ceased to amaze me, because despite being an ugly duckling, her redeeming facet was that she was very well-read and highly cerebral, managing to captivate the most eligible bachelor-industrialist of the last century for quite a few years.

Sadly, he too died on her some years later, after consummating a sunset fling in his last phase of life with her.

I didn't like her because she was judgemental, a voyeur who enjoyed gossiping about others' lives as she didn't have one of her own. I overheard her tell Maasi, 'Your niece from Calcutta is attractive. I hear she's making waves in Delhi and women are a bit intimidated with her arrival here because she's single, Indira.'

Maasi's family honour was at stake, so she snubbed Sulochana and rubbished her innuendo. 'So?! Yes, my niece is single. But she's not on the prowl, I assure you. Besides, Sulochana, she's entitled to explore her options morally, being formally divorced. These days I know of miserable marriages that last not out of affinity but more out of dire need. Spouses who just suffer each other even if they share nothing in common. At least my Akshraa decided to give her marriage many tries but didn't make a mockery of wedlock by two-timing her husband.'

I heard that a great argument ensued on the subject between the two, short of Maasi snubbing Sulochana on how immoral she was to have cuckolded her rich and aged husband. But Indira abstained from pushing it, as she was the hostess, and refrained from entering into an unpleasant verbal duel with her guest after concluding an afternoon of playing bridge.

I got an inkling of a very catty, harsh and judgmental society out here, full of duplicity. As I became more confident in my skin, I learned to rebut, as equally respect those who were more benign and accepting of human frailties.

My greatest mentor-cum-friend-cum-ally was Tina, a teenage association since my LSR days. Though she was my lifeline, she was also a walking talking Wikipedia in her prolific knowledge on anything ranging from fashion, to sports, to politics, to the economy. Full of positive energy, she must have been gifted with dollops of endorphins since she was on a perpetual high. Over time, I trusted her wisdom to navigate my way through turbulent times, as she became the moral compass I could consult on the most intimate questions that disturbed me. Reviving a friendship with a college friend felt good as we had evolved and grown at the same pace, and in a new city it was comforting having an old friendship devoid of competitiveness or judgement. As she had also kept up with Maasi, I was pleasantly surprised to meet up with her after years at my aunt's home and revive a strong bond that lasted a lifetime.

Later in the evening, I was introduced to Aslam Khan, a tall and handsome son of a cabinet minister, who I was told lived off the wealth of his lineage but made little of his own. They owned a business in meat exports and the scion indulged in hawala trading on the side, for which he came under scrutiny many years after his father lost power. He was supposed to have been a part of the ruling family's coterie at that time, conscious that he derived proxy-power by virtue of his proximity to 'Auntie's son', Auntie being Indira Gandhi.

A finesse and speaking style that came from pedigree eluded him, almost like he never made it through a finishing school to polish and complete him. The poor guy stammered while talking, and that made him seem a little less intimidating and little less fierce.

Aslam Khan had come to Maasi's party to fill in for his dad, who was held up at a cabinet meeting. He appeared to be in his mid-forties, supported a stubble that looked like he hadn't shaved for a few days, and possessed sharp features like an Afghani. Brash in his mannerisms, he thought little of editing his four-letter cuss words. Strangely, that was also his charm. I believed he would make a very good friend but a bad enemy. He was aloof and hardly mingled that evening, heading towards a tête-a-tête with a retired Colonel, who was now an arms dealer, with whom he seemed to share a comfortable bonhomie. I saw them huddled in a corner, Aslam downing a few quick, neat shots of vodka, his eyes taking on a tinge of red, while the Colonel seemed to be on attendance to Khan. He was known as 'Mr 2 per cent', as he front-ended for his father in transacting defence deals.

Serious negotiations seemed to be on between the Colonel and Khan, till he got abusive with the latter all of a sudden, caught him by the collar and dragged him out to the garden that the drawing room opened on to. Apparently the Colonel had condemned Indira Gandhi's regime of excesses and her curtailment of civil liberties, telling Aslam how people resented Mrs Gandhi's autocratic rule; the colonel felt he knew Khan well enough to give his political take by way of a harmless drawing-room conversation. 'Colonel, if you step out of line, I will get Abbu to cancel the contract,' Khan threatened.

His wife rushed out in an attempt to douse the sudden outburst. His entourage of chamchas followed suit, requesting, 'Bhabhi, please don't come outside. We are here to attend on Khan sahib.' The Colonel seemed desperate to pacify Khan, apologizing for no fault of his, knowing he had too much to lose should the inebriated Khan get even angrier. Pin-drop silence descended for a few minutes, as sounds of Khan's rants could be heard inside the drawing room. Conversation had ceased, the noise of the melee drowning the clamour of the chatterati inside the room. Maasi also rushed out to the garden in order to appease her VIP guest. Khan brusquely elbowed his hostess aside and said, 'Indira, next time you invite the likes of this Colonel, count Najma and me out.'

Taking up cudgels with a political heavyweight could land one in trouble in those days. If not imprisonment (as the colonel was no political opponent or someone of stature), the harassment of an income tax raid was a possible consequence of intimidating a political goon.

~

Most people I met when I was in and out of my aunt's house were very closely aligned to the Sanjay Gandhi camp. But by the time I had shifted to Delhi for good, the Sanjay brigade was weakened and scattered after his premature demise.

Past midnight, after dinner was nearly over, in walked an unmistakably recognizable face to join my aunt's party for just a Cointreau. She breezed in wearing a backless choli, bejewelled in a stunning four-string South Sea pearl necklace with a diamond clasp on one side. Rather elegant, she warranted a second look with her translucent complexion. That was Rukshana Sultana, the notorious socialite-cum-social worker and a part of Sanjay Gandhi's innermost coterie during 1976, when 'the glamour girl of Emergency' was on the headlines of every newspaper for her infamous role in supervising the demolition of shops in the Turkaman Gate area. As Rukshana strutted around the slums of Jama Masjid she was rumoured to be holding a perfumed kerchief to her nose to drown out the stench of poverty, wearing her signature-style oversized Channel sunshades. She was supposed to have been awarded a sum of ₹84,000, a princely payout those days, by the union health and family welfare ministry for 'motivating' eight thousand men to opt for vasectomies, as an acknowledgment for her exemplary service to the nation!

Of course, she incurred the wrath of Muslims for implementing Sanjay Gandhi's family planning programme, as much as incurred the ire of the poor for the demolitions at Turkman Gate. During the Emergency, Indira Gandhi's government, prompted by her son Sanjay, launched the demolition drive to cleanse Delhi of slums, demolishing hutments with bulldozers, which forced their poor residents to relocate to distant settlements.

Her antecedents kept me staring at her in wonderment, awestruck by her grace and power-talk that hadn't yet waned, for her well-known proximity to Sanjay Gandhi, India's de facto prime minister those years. Even years past the Emergency, I saw her obsequiously felicitated upon her entrance at my aunt's house by two business magnates who, I was told, were trying to cosy up to her for clearance of their licences stuck in red-tape bureaucratic hurdles, because some felt she still had inroads to Mrs G, as she kept up that façade of holding power even years after Sanjay Gandhi's demise.

❧

But who I loved most was Auntie Guddi. At a charity fashion soiree, I saw her elegantly pirouette across the ramp as blithely as a breeze, as artistically as a ballet dancer, nimble-footed in her killer stilettoes. She must have been in her fifties, her hair streaked with salt-and-pepper strands, but I had heard she was something of a soignée swan in her twenties. Poised and immaculately silhouetted, her skin had a porcelain texture, so translucent that you could almost see a mirror reflection of your visage on her complexion. She feigned being vulnerable in the presence of men, a feminine attribute they found so seductive that it elicited a protective instinct in them to hold, cajole or caress her.

Auntie Guddi was my icon in Delhi, beautiful and completely devoted to her husband, gracious and oh-so-very feminine! If she was a femme fatale in her time, big deal! Her husband doted on her to the extreme that he was fiercely possessive, stifling her fun-loving side. I had heard she was the belle-of-the-ball in her earlier years and had settled for a passing fling with her Guru as she grew deeper into the world of religion. But over the years she had found her balance between the material and the spiritual, loving her broccoli boiled, her asparagus in Hollaindaise sauce, her truffles black and her politics saffron!

She owned a grand hotel and lived out of a palatial suite, her lifestyle attracting an eclectic draw of Delhi's biggies. Her guest lists included artists, thinkers, corporate honchos, ministers, industrialists or even Kathakali danseuses and brigadiers from the armed forces.

At one of her cocktails I overheard an industrialist telling another, 'Didn't see you at Davos this year, Mannu?'

After a sip of his Bourbon on the rocks, the other took a long pause and replied, 'Yaar, I had to sign a big collaboration in New York, so missed the event. I've been a regular at Davos, but never seen you attend in the previous years?'

I reckoned a game of one-upmanship was on between the tycoons, so after being introduced to both of them, I felt left out of the conversation and moved aside.

Holding fort at the opposite corner of the room was a khadi-clad politician in Bally shoes, telling a fair-skinned adman who was reputed to belong to Rajiv Gandhi's inner circle, '...as I was telling the head of the Finance Commission and members of the CBDT...'

His listener, who looked disinterested and bored, cut short his flamboyance and quipped, 'You know, I got a call from Mrs G last night to meet up with her at 11. She wanted to consult me at that late hour about how to revamp the image of the Congress being perceived as anti-Muslim and regain the support of the community after the nasbundi-forced sterilization cases and the demolition of Turkman Gate hutments...So was up till late... I haven't slept a wink...' Mr Show-off No. 2 obviously held sway... his pomposity outdoing Mr Show-off No. 1. Power, power, and more power! This was what the city was about. Fascinating and equally intimidating to a new entrant.

∾

While I had left behind a promiscuous city, as Calcutta was in the 80s, I realized the upper crust of Delhi was no different. Except that the pace of life was faster as people lived more affluent lives, having exposure to better opportunities; and instead of the softer arts of literature, culture and sports, politics and hardcore 'deal-making' dominated drawing-room conversations. Being the capital and the centre of power, proximity to the Gandhis or their coterie defined social prominence which was au naturel.

Initially I was in awe of this new world, its people and the city. I hated it. I hated their arrogance, their volatility, their fierceness, where innocent arguments could flare into ire. It disturbed my delicate sensitivity as I had never witnessed anything of this sort in the cultured city I had come from. But with the passage of time, I knew no other way of being...becoming like any one of them, as Delhi became my home.

In Search of an Identity

'All answers lie embedded in your inner wisdom.
Stand up and express the divinity within you.'
—Swami Vivekananda

I LANDED A plum job at Taj Hotel, since I possessed a fair amount of marketing skills. The love of my life, Vishal, my prince, was sent to an elite boarding school in Sanawar, in the verdant Kasauli hills, so he could be cocooned from the vicissitudes of his mother's life... It wrenched my heart as I only got to see glimpses of my only child's growing years on intermittent holidays. If there was any collateral damage that I suffered as a consequence of my derailed life, it was the guilt of an unimaginable velocity that gnawed at my heart night after night, of being a single parent.

It was in the dew of little joys that my heart found its mornings, as my world revolved around little Vishal and providing him all that money could buy to make up for all else I deprived him of. I earned for him, I lived for him. He was my world.

That became my motto to live and die by and somewhere it diminished the guilt of being separated from this godlike, innocent child. I tried hard to make up for my lapses at parenting, those unpardonable errors of my insensitive, self-obsessed, foolish twenties. I am not sure I had managed to erase hurtful memories of his childhood by offering perfect parenthood to Vishal in his thirties, when it was least needed for survival for a lad who had by now transited into manhood. Too little, too late it was, as by the time realization dawned, he had grown into a fine, well-integrated young man. But I did my best! I truly did try to make amends. I dare say his childhood scars must have remained at a subconscious level, but he concealed them beautifully.

It was a strange comfort that when Obama visited India in 2015, I heard him say, as a tribute to his mother, that he was proud of his country that gave 'the son of a single mother' the opportunity to scale such heights. It mildly absolved me of the self-recriminating, self-flagellating thoughts I harboured for three decades of blaming myself for depriving Vishal of the wholeness a growing child feels of owning both a mother and a father.

∾

At work by nine in the morning, I would arrive at the hotel in a whispery chiffon saree and a string of pearls to work with passion. Actually, it became my raison d'être, as I thought of my job as a hobby, a fun activity, not pressured by any need to earn a living even when I worked in Calcutta. 'Love what you do, and you will never feel you worked a single day in your life,' Warren Buffet's inspirational words rang in my mind.

My day started with a dip in the Jacuzzi in the health spa at Taj. Mellow music, dimly lit with just the flicker of candles, cobalt blue mosaic tiles…this little haven was the place I ideated my most creative thoughts for the day. Jyoti, my colleague, who was also at the spa said, 'You realize you and I need to be ready to submit our detailed business plans to the chairman before noon? Any thoughts, Akshraa?'

'Nope! Jyoti, heaven can wait! But till I am not done with the whirlpool, the windmills of my mind will not churn. Give me a while, I am still foggy. I think I will be able to brainstorm some facts and figures for the plan with you shortly. Have faith, we will give them a plan that will blow their minds.'

And we did! We strategized how to corner 76 per cent of the market share; it was a near-reality. In those days I possessed the singularity of purpose of a zealot, coupled with a childlike surety that anything I wanted and focused on had to come my way! Wasn't the world my oyster?

~

Four decades later, as a woman who was imparted the basics of a sound education and average common sense, I can say with certitude that when work and exercise are pursued with passion and fun, they become a prayerful reverie and ritual. No downturns in life can then shake one as they both become a pivotal force, a 'constant' amidst a life of variables.

Work then was my prayer, my hobby, my drug. The love of labour filled the vacuum in my life as the years went by.

Close Encounters with an Ignited Mind

FEW ARE PRIVILEGED to participate in a modest start-up of the 1980s that grew into a legendary behemoth, with a net worth of $14 billion by 2015. I am, of course, talking about HCL. Within a span of less than three decades, this was remarkable by any performance paradigm. It was in 1983, during my most formative and impressionable years, that I was mentored by a luminary of our times, Shiv Nadar. I did not realize then how this phase of my life was to form the bedrock of wisdom and experience that shielded me through vicissitudes in the years to come.

A man of few words and serious demeanour, he was one of the pioneers of the New Age industry of information technology. It was globally the third wave of evolution as world economies transited from industrial to information- and knowledge-based industries.

I watched the man's meteoric ascent, his vision statement even at that time bordering on paranoia and a laser beam precision at implementation. 'Some men see things as they are, and ask why? I dream of things that never were, and ask why not?'

Nadar's success lay in converging skill sets, bringing together a set of experts from finance, technology, HR and marketing to constitute an entrepreneurial company. This start-up then was born of a seed capital of ideas and expertise more than the limited financial seed capital it invested. Even though this was during the pre-liberalization, licence-raj era, the ethics and principles of corporate governance that percolated top-down raised the bar of morality in this small emerging organization.

The industry was at a very nascent, experimental stage, highly attrition-prone as professionals jumped ship frequently. But Shiv had great intuition in spotting and sustaining talent, turning almost proprietorial as he watched his prodigies grow into super-achievers, short of patenting them!

Nadar had formulated generous performance-linked incentives, laddered upwards, measuring man–month–productivity in quantifiable ways in order to measure and reward achievements. So, not only did my salary increase rapidly, helping me build assets, this enabled my team to be inclusive in partaking of the 'intrapeneurs' module Nadar was experimenting with those days. It was a concept when employees working as heads of a vertical grew organically to achieve virtual ownership under the umbrella of an entrepreneur. In this mode, an employee determined the risk-reward as a mini stakeholder for himself. It compelled the task force to remain ahead of the curve, there being no scope for mediocrity or you ran the risk of turning dead-wood-redundant sooner than you could imagine.

I headed a vertical called 'Oscar'. The name was almost prophetic in what my team set out to achieve: 'The future belonged to people who believed in the power of their dreams.' Monthly meetings were goal-setting agendas for the next three months and you were only as good as your performance in the last quarter. As an exercise addict feels only as good as his or her last workout, it was the same with quantifying the deliverables at work here.

For some reason, Shiv took a near-sadistic thrill in setting the tallest targets for this vertical. 'Akshraa, your team has to deliver 10 crores sales by the end of the year. We can't revise this figure or negotiate on it. If anything, that's the floor, that's the base. Let's talk upwards from here, got it?'

'You're kidding. Do you know, Mr Nadar, we don't match half the specifications of government tenders. Our after-sales support is not well equipped in the remote corners where Coal India's operations are located to service them, leading to a 'downtime' of operational efficiency, for example.'

I was going to carry on with my list of excuses on why this humongous target was unachievable when he stopped me in my tracks. 'A bad man blames his tools. OSCAR can do it…', saying that, he strutted off but I got the drift. In this industry, I learned early that one couldn't rest on past laurels, as one had to remain in one's discomfort zone to stay relevant. The organization compelled one to learn to be responsive, agile and resilient to the rapid pace of transformations. I began to thrive on deriving my professional competence from a space of curiosity rather than fear.

At a personal level, creative thinking mobilized me into being unafraid of rejections or self-doubt, no matter what circumstances I confronted. Nadar, who matured into the visionary of today, was at that time the poster boy of start-ups in the 1980s, what brash e-commerce entrepreneurs like Flipkart's Sachin Bansal or a Kunal Bahl of Snapdeal are to the New Age economy, striving to take their ventures to billion-dollar valuations in quick time.

My experience at HCL compelled me to learn how to brace disruptions way back in the '80s, albeit they were less rapid then as compared to the turn of the century, as one learned to recognize how to live with this reality of the 'new normal'.

The transition from the mainframe computers of the '60s to the personal computer of the '80s was not such a quantum leap in technology as are innovations and disruptions to the smartphones and tablets category in recent years. Obsolescence was gradual in the earlier years of the IT industry. Confronting rapid challenges in a dynamically changing work environment wired my mind at a subconscious level to deal with transience in my personal space going forward, instead of being intimidated or fearful of flux.

In my learning curve with HCL, however, what struck me as rarest of rare was the 'philanthro-capitalism' by the turn of the century of nearly every tech trillionaire in India and abroad. Economic history had never seen first-generation self-made entrepreneurs generous enough to gift away their self-made fortunes to the exclusion of silver-spoon inheritance passed on traditionally only to their offspring. While Bill Gates and Mark Zuckerberg pledged more than half their fortunes to the underprivileged, back home their Indian counterparts Narayan Murthy, Nadar and Azim Premji were trending the same module of giving away to the less fortunate in preference over their progeny. India's super-haves displayed a callous vulgarity in their excesses, living the life of 'robber barons' as a consequence of unchecked capitalism, to the exclusion of working towards a more equitable society. The disparity of the '1 per cent being wealthier than the have-not 99 per cent' was glaring, as equally distressing. This economic disparity is the central thought in economist Thomas Piketty's watershed book, *Capital in the Twenty-First Century*, wherein he vents about the evils of unrestrained capitalism that created more inequality than growth, as the affluent defined themselves with in-your-face lifestyles. While it was hypocrisy to think of possessing excessive wealth as a sin, politicians and governments the world over favoured a system that perpetuated a compounding monopoly of resources in the hands of the rich, complicit in cronyism with industrial lobbies in a cosy exchange for favours.

The philanthro-capitalist model of the IT industry made me acutely aware that each of us in our individual capacity needed to rethink our responsibility towards society in proportion to our earnings, in whatever minuscule way we could.

Risk-taking, creativity and a free flow of ideas thrived within HCL where interactions with the boss were flat and non-hierarchical, where great ideas were rewarded. It was a daring adventure where paragliding the skies of ambition spiked its own adrenalin high, when you knew your boss was there to back you for a soft landing. Nadar and I had struck a magical working synergy because he knew how to grab the big idea when he spotted one and I had the manic obssessiveness to go after it.

The career choice was to brave it between an established business house, of the Tatas, which was ranked amongst the top two of the country versus a near-start-up those days. But the lightness of being a beginner was supported financially and emotionally to such an extent that it freed me to enter the most creative period of my life. I was unafraid from thereon. From an accidental professional I had become an accidental investor, to building a corpus in real estate in later years by just taking small steps towards feeling financially self-sufficient. I felt good with my modest achievements then, though they were not fantabulous. It is only years later when I looked back in time that I was able to connect the dots of how my life and achievements were actually forming a base for the future, rather than splintering my life apart. It was forming the bedrock of something so solid that it empowered me for the rest of my life.

∾

I had gotten over the human need of feeling complete only if one was in a relationship. Working in a surcharged atmosphere at HCL with the superlative energy of bright and young entrepreneurs surrounding me became my world. Working to optimal capacity gave me the same human emotions of reward and a sense of self-worth, not dependent on someone else but one that stemmed from my own creativity and grit.

Part II

Finding Love Again

Surya and I: The Courtship Years

1987

I FIRST MET Suryaprakash at the age of thirty-one, not young enough for insta-loving, but more like love at second sight. A common friend from Chennai was dropping in for a casual dinner. As Neeraj Gupta was informal enough with me to bring along a close friend, he took the liberty to bring his best buddy, Surya Mittal, along to spend the evening at my house. I had read about this business magnate in newspapers from time to time, how ahead of the curve and visionary he was in having grown his empire completely on his own steam, despite being a scion of one of the most affluent business families. He came across as rather shy, unaffected by his success, and utterly humble, despite being amongst the top ten names in industry those years. I made little of it then, talking on neutral topics of the day like politics and exchanging pleasantries as a hostess. He was merely a very good friend of another good friend, so I just extended the normal courtesies one does to any guest coming over for potluck.

Some months passed by till we chanced to meet again at a party, from where be picked up the threads of the last meeting at my house. We met over a one-on-one dinner he invited me to in a restaurant on the rooftop of the Taj. Very formal, very correct, as I made little of a dinner with a first time acquaintance.

Many more months passed, though he did call a few times in between to keep the connect, as I responded with the same lightheartedness, making little of it still.

Over time, the meetings became more frequent. I guess I was lonely, introspective and responsive too, open to meeting someone I was beginning to find a comfort level with. I was never too fond of partying or late nights, as I loved my work at HCL and looked forward to waking up fresh to go to office the next day. So romance or finding love again was least on my mind. A serious relationship with any man was farthest from my priorities, as I was on such a high with my work, having numbed my emotions. Earning a livelihood and making something of my life consumed my time much more than any other frivolous pursuits.

~

I got to know a little more about Suryaprakash, the man, his mind and his family values, more as a very good friend-in-the-making, over the random meetings and chats we had over eight or nine months. At that time, Mittal's conglomerate was considered to be one of the most reputed Indian industrial houses, with market leadership in many business verticals including cement, fertilizers, infrastructure and media. After graduating from Harvard Business School, Surya told me how he had worked his way up, interning within the family businesses as Executive Assistant to the Finance Director in one of his grandfather's companies, and later becoming the President of this leading group, when he expanded the company into sectors of real-estate development and media.

But soon after the demise of his grandfather, who was the founder of the group, he ventured into his own business deciding to tough it out as a totally self-made entrepreneur, despite being born into a privileged life.

He went on to tell me interesting anecdotes from time to time of how, when he was studying at Harvard, his grandfather offered this advice to him in a letter: 'Eat only vegetarian food, never drink alcohol or smoke, sleep early, wake up before sunrise, marry before you are twenty-four (and don't bring back a girl from the West as our bahu), switch off lights when leaving the room, cultivate discipline, meditate daily, and above all, don't be extravagant.' All this sounded so familiar to what my father, rooted in middle-class values, would lecture his two daughters about the virtues of simplicity, so typical of that era.

Mittal senior also instructed his grandson to never utilize wealth only for 'fun and frolic', and to practice frugality, 'spending the bare minimum on yourself and more on the poor', and to relinquish 'worldly pleasures by the age of fifty'. The advice symbolized the ethics of restraint and austerity that Surya's father had already begun to follow upon Dada ji's commands, having retired from business by middle age, and started living in Benares mostly, pursuing religious studies, more or less relinquishing his family life, and having minimal material needs. Sanyasa was traditionally conceptualized in our scriptures for men or women in the late years of their life, after being a householder, transiting to a retirement stage, and ultimately renouncing worldly and materialistic pursuits so as to dedicate their lives towards attaining 'moksha'.

Our connection at the outset was a highly cerebral one in the initial months before hearts met. A physical lure was farthest from our minds as emotions only grew with time because an amour second time around is seldom as instantaneous or innocent as in one's teens. He acknowledged my worth as amongst a rare breed of working women in those years, so Surya loved telling me about his world of business as much as I enjoyed listening to his stories or telling him about the challenges of the IT industry in its nascent days. It grew into an emotional attachment over time as we began to meet almost every day.

Being too prudish and rooted in middle-class values, I prided myself in not getting swayed by his wealth or power to sell my soul for the brevity of a passing fascination or a foolish favour. Owning a comfortable quotient through my earnings and also fortunately backed by sound assets through my lineage, I did not succumb to being swept off my feet irrationally. Surya was too noble to exploit me even if, as an older and more experienced man, he sensed my latent scars or baggage of the past. Neither did he carry much emotional baggage from his first marriage into the present.

One day he asked if I would like to accompany him on a whirlwind business tour to Geneva, proceeding on to New York. 'The trip is on me, Akshraa. I would love you to come. We will be back in just five days. Are you game?'

My first reaction was feeling cheap at his extending this generous offer. I wanted to accompany him but didn't relish the idea of being obliged for my bill being picked up. If anything, I was peeved. Self-righteous, and on a high moral ground, I didn't want to feel like I had a price, that I was being bought over. 'Surya, thanks. I am tempted to accompany you abroad, but I can afford this trip on my own.' I lied, because I had never travelled first-class ever before, since it was too exorbitant for a working-class person, nor could I really afford this trip by paying cash. Go I did by calling up my travel agent and paying for my trip in instalments. EMIs were non-existent those years.

'So do I instruct my office to book a separate room for you,

Akshraa, as you have declined my desire to pay for your travel expenses too?'

'No. There's no need for that. I will happily stay with you in your presidential suite.'

'Strange! Akshraa, you confound me with your logic. You won't let me pay for your airfare, so do tell me why is it you don't mind the "obligation" of living with me in the same room? It doesn't make sense.'

'Ha ha! Let me answer your question with glee, Mr Mittal. Surya, the difference between the rate of single or double occupancy is the cost of a drink or two. That honour I don't mind conferring on you and partaking of your largesse, you being the man in my life. That's a trivial nicety, and I would love to be indulged with your offer, quite honestly, as it doesn't compromise my femininity nor my pride one bit.'

It was a pleasurable five days of bonding, as Surya had business meets lined up during the day while in the evenings we dined together. It also gave one space, vital to any thriving relationship. But for the last evening... He returned at 10.30 in the night without even phoning to tell me he would be late. 'Honey, sorry but I couldn't wrap it up earlier, as Eva Menzes, the daughter of my collaborator, insisted I have a drink with her after the meeting ended. I have known her parents for some years and she wanted to talk to me about a problem with her marriage. I just thought it was obligatory on my part not to decline...' Strange! Couldn't he have included me in the evening half of the program knowing I was all alone through the day? As I sprung up from my sofa to greet him, I got a whiff of an awfully potent fragrance of Opium, a distinctly feminine aroma that lingered on him. I must be imagining, I felt... I guess he really couldn't get to a phone and meeting Eva over a drink was just a business nicety. Why make much of it and ruin a first holiday together! Silly me! He wouldn't have got me to accompany him overseas if he had a hidden agenda, I felt.

This was my first induction into living life the Mittal way, in a grandiose presidential suite within which my entire home in Golf Links would have fitted. Unimaginable opulence. I had never before lived a life of such luxury as I did in those four nights. I lost my heart on this trip to Surya but hoped being indulged in such luxury I would never lose my soul too someday. In the silence of my being as I was falling asleep, I prayed to God, 'Lord, I thank you for this bountiful experience of seeing a world I never knew. May I never lose my innocence to this fairy-tale world Surya has given me a glimpse of and grow to love the man for what he is, not for who he is.'

I woke up the next morning with a gift Surya had placed under my pillow. A beautifully wrapped gold-and-diamond chain from Tiffany's, which I constantly wore from then on as my 'mangalsutra', emblematic of a married woman's pride around her neck as long as she lived. Except this was a Western love necklace that weighed heavy on my slender neck because I felt deeply obligated for such an expensive gift.

I was grateful as much as I was beholden. Truly, I had never been a recipient of such munificence.

This was just to be the beginning of a fairy-tale romance. It didn't end there. On our last night in Geneva, we went down to the hotel bar to enjoy a sundowner, followed by early dinner at the hotel's fine-dining rooftop restaurant. We were too tired to step out, as we had an early morning flight on the Concorde to New York the following morning.

'Some champagne today, Akshraa? You are just going to love your first experience aboard the supersonic jet. You may not enjoy the luxury of space within the aircraft, as you did in first-class travelling, because it's a very narrow-bodied jet with limited leg space, but you will enjoy the speed of travel to get to your destination in half the time. Let's start the eve of the next leg of our journey with a glass of bubbly in anticipation, shall we?'

'No, Surya...please, not for me. I don't mind a Capriochka though; you can have the champagne,' I said.

He had already told the bartender to serve us a flute each, so I didn't quite have a choice. The waiter poured us both glasses of Dom Pérignon. Surya extended one first to me—a tall-stemmed glass which had a stunning ring studded with champagne-diamonds lying at the bottom. I had only seen images of this exotic diamond, though never in real life. Staring disbelievingly at what was presented to me, utterly stupefied and awestruck, my jaws opened wide as I struck my hand to my mouth, utterly flummoxed, thinking for a moment : 'Had some absent-minded, eccentric richie-rich left this ornate piece by mistake at the bar? What was this being served up before me?' It took me a few seconds to make sense of the surprise Surya meant to overwhelm me with. He gently pulled the ring out from the glass, delving through the dancing froth of sparkling champagne, and slipped it on my finger.

This was a surreal day in my life, when I woke up with a diamond and ended the day being pampered with this ring.

Was I sipping diamonds for real? Or was it a dream?

Meeting the Rajmata

December 1988

ON A COLD and frosty morning in December 1988, Surya lovingly summoned me to have a formal meeting with Amma ji.

I tossed and turned the night before, anxious—would I be able to strike a chord and gain her approval? I understood from Surya's cousin Ruchika that Amma ji hailed from the erstwhile princely family of Punjab, having married into the true blue-blooded royalty of one of the first families of Indian industry when she was just sixteen. Though Indira Gandhi had abolished privy purses years back that saw the end of royalty, these families still retained their traditions in grooming their girls in poise, finesse and French, as an unmistakable air of grandeur was a hallmarked trait all the way. Amma ji, I was told, also owned those attributes of grace, having studied at St Joseph's Convent in Punjab, visiting and doing 'sewa' at the Golden Temple as often as she could and heading multiple charities for the underprivileged at gurdwaras. Being a Sikh, she felt deeply for the plight of the '84 riot victims, and involved herself as an active crusader for their cause, being of noble disposition. It somewhat quelled my anxiousness when I learnt that she was kind and charitable and not forbidding, but nothing prepared me for the aristocratic arrogance of the lady.

The Mittals owned multiple businesses in undivided India, their industries based out of Chiniot, having interests in sugar and textiles pre-Partition. Babu ji, while studying in the Government College, Lahore, used to cycle across on weekends to meet Amma ji in Amritsar, once the families had approved of each other. Babu ji and Amma ji may not have been from the same state or religion, but their families were of a similar league in status, besides having a comfort level due to a long association with each other over two generations. Besides, I was told by Ruchi, the two families had felt that it would be a great match of old money with old class. Knowing a bit about the background, I was kind of comfortable as I felt there would be so much to talk in a free flow of preliminary niceties.

Nervous and in awe, my mane in pigtails, wearing a salwaar kameez, I was driven to Mittal House in my modest Fiat by my driver the next morning. The lush verdant pathways into its sprawling acres within Lutyens' Delhi, known as the Millionaires Avenue of Asia, were in close proximity to where I lived.

The porch was populated by some thirty limousines of every shape, colour and make. Their home, an opulent ornate baroque style, had a very formal feel from the very first step. The entrance to the house appeared like the busy reception area of a grand hotel, as a team of telephone operators went about their work. Surya was waiting at the foyer to welcome me into his awe-inspiring, unfamiliar terrain as I arrived.

He half-embraced me as I entered within view of the receptionists, so we didn't quite give each other that affectionate bear hug as when we met alone. 'Akshraa, Amma is running late as she's still doing her puja. Let's chat till then in my TV room. You look so tense, chill, bachiyaa! You have only arrived in a home that will be yours soon. I know my mother will just love you.' That was so utterly endearing and assuring. He always called me 'bachiyaa', as he told me lovingly he found my nature as docile and meek as a baby calf. Alas! How I wish I could have retained that docility over the years, because my personality underwent multiple somersaults as I went through life with him.

In walked Hari, his Man Friday, with two tall glasses of freshly squeezed pomegranate juice. I later learned to my utter amusement that among Hari's duties towards Surya, one was to taste the seasonal fruit and approve it, informing his majesty if it was ripe/khatta/mitha or whatever. I was tickled pink when Hari was once on leave after we got married and Surya said to me, 'Bachiyaa, can you please taste this alphonso that's come from Mumbai and tell me if its sweet enough?' I honestly didn't know whether to laugh, cry or just peck him on the cheek for his spoilt-brattish behaviour.

Before escorting me into the room of the Rajmata, his queen mother, he made me feel at ease, sensing my apologetic lack of Hindi-speaking skills that might embarrass either his mother or myself, by telling me, 'Relax, Aksh, don't fret, your meeting will go well. She is fluent in English, being convent-educated like you. Aksh, your winning ways will endear you to her. She is a very simple person.'

I requested Surya, 'Then please will you introduce us, deposit me with her and then leave us alone on some pretext so I am not doubly conscious in your presence to open up to her?' To which he smiled indulgently, nodded and did the needful, before driving off for office.

As I was ushered into this long, though informal, study room with a huge depth, Amma sat perched at the far end on a regal silver throne amidst a very British-looking library with green leather-bound books. The cacophony of birds from the garden was the only noise one heard in a home inhabited by so many people. The liveried staff traipsed noiselessly, carrying bite-sized dosas and khandvi to serve some guests being entertained by a family member in the adjoining formal drawing room. I reckoned a business meeting was in progress there.

The manor had a beautiful fragrance of sandalwood wafting through the air, reminding me that I was inside a home that was deeply religious and traditional, that performed ritualistic pujas round the clock. There were two full-time pujaris whose only job was to pray, bathe and feed the gods, I was told. 'But Surya, why are paid priests needed to bathe the gods and recite proxy-prayers on behalf of your family members? Can't you clean and dust the images yourself, recite a short and meaningful prayer and get going with the day?'

I wondered whether the fraternity of godhood could be appeased with less formality, by an innocent heart and good deeds, or was all this fuss and ceremony more important to ingratiate and please them in heaven? I always found a certain monotony and fakeness in the practice of rituals of formal religion.

If only Surya or Amma ji could hear my inner dialogue, I would have been condemned for blasphemy and heresy by the family I wanted to marry into, deemed an errant kafir or a wayward infidel! His father was the illustrious head of the sanctimonious BHS, the Bharatiya Hind Sanstha, one of the many ideological fountainheads and offshoots of the right-winged BJP. A proponent of the Ram Mandir and a committed activist for its resurrection to reinstate Hindu garv was his passionate cause. Sadly, I was told, Pita ji and Surya had momentary temperamental differences, so they were in a sulk with each other for now.

However distanced Surya was from Pita ji, his strong

Hindutva-BHS inculcation prevailed deeply on his beliefs and mannerisms. This was in sharp contrast to the thoroughbred convent educated woman that I was, who enjoyed Christmas as a child, writing letters to Santa Claus asking for Barbie dolls dressed in pink cancans and frocks, and relished turkey lunches and plum puddings, where even my jesting about it with Surya elicited a frown.

But Surya did successfully peddle some of the families ossified traditions on to me over the years. I recall being a trifle bemused when on my first birthday he celebrated, as I was about to blow out the candles on the cake, he mildly chided me, 'Akshraa, when we are born, each of us brings light as we illumine the world. It's only in the West that people snuff out candles. Please appreciate our Hindu tradition and never blow out the light.' I thought that was an unusual and pristine thought and way of looking at the event, so I decided to follow suit and obey him.

Leapfrog to 2014, the year BJP was firmly in governance and out to alter our perspectives in auguring a revival of our culture and tradition. Dina Nath Batra was popularizing the same tradition, 'Why do we cut cakes on birthdays and blow out candles? Why do we celebrate Valentine's Day or accept chocolates from Santa Claus?' I wondered in jest whether these mascots and proponents of our revivalism would make it mandatory for Santa to distribute laddoos in lieu of Western toffees in the future, or would he now have to arrive in a dhoti kurta? For the uninitiated, Batra was the zealous historian who, after successfully sabotaging Wendy Doniger's book on Hinduism, was made out to be the ultimate Superman of Hinduism and began rewriting history.

I realized I would have to indigenize my thought patterns to fit into the traditional home that I had set foot in if I wanted to be accepted within the family fold.

❧

Amma ji, I was told, was very pretty in her youth and retained a royal air about her still. She was deeply religious and charitable, but a firm no-nonsense matriarch. Attired in a subtle white-and-gold traditional tanchoi saree, she was adorned with serious solitaires on her ears like knuckledusters. She appeared stern in her highly powered specs that slipped midway to her nose, her gaze piercing as I entered her room. Her aura was unmistakably forbidding. As cold as the rocks that adorned her, a bit aloof and distant in her body language, yet fairly old-world grace, were the vibes I got from her as I nervously dived to touch her feet with a reverent 'pranaam'. I could barely hear my own oblation, overcome as I was with fear and awe of the formidable lady's aura.

She moved her feet away as I bent to touch them, saying, '*Iski koi zaroorat nahi hai*,' dismissing my reverence curtly. Was I being hypersensitive, imagining her aloofness? I couldn't tell.

'Amma ji, I was looking forward to meeting with you...aapka kamra bahut tastefully done up hai. You have a fine collection of antiques and Tanjore paintings that must have taken you years to accumulate?' I queried.

'*Aap Amma mat kahiye*. You can call me Mrs Mittal or Auntie,' rebuking my attempt at even a remote proximity on breaking any formal barriers.

The air was strictly formal as she half-smiled with a kind of condescension that made me feel as small as Dimple Kapadia must have felt as a teenage girl in the film *Bobby*, being confronted by the boy's arrogant and contemptuous parents. I sat down on the green Chesterfield sofa, holding both my hands in a semi-prayerful way as she proceeded to inquisition me, '*So, aap kya kartey hain, Akshraa?*' avoiding the niceties that go with a preliminary first meet with elders but looking pointedly into my eyes. I shivered as though I was being screened by a schoolmarm.

I soon shed my awkwardness and put myself at ease even if she was not going to shed her semi-hostile demeanour. I had no defences to shield myself from her glacial sparks. I believed I was invited to pay my respects to an elder who I thought would be a kind, affectionate, jovial auntie ji. I was here to be introduced to the love of my life's mother and though she was the matriarch of her royal family, I was not seeking to procure a job or be overtly subservient even though I wanted to marry Suryaprakash.

Tense moments took the mickey out of me! My innate naiveté that stemmed from my simplicity became my strength and provided the armour to shield me as I replied with contrived confidence, 'Me! Uhh, Mrs Mittal, I work for a living in a computer company, which is a start-up.' I continued my monologue out of utter nervousness, though unasked, 'My father is a senior bureaucrat based in Mumbai and Mummy is a practising lawyer, Auntie ji.'

'So they must be living in good government-provided staff housing?'

'Jee nahi, Auntie. They live on Cuffe Parade.'

'Rented flat, I suppose?'

'Not at all, Auntie. They invested in a beautiful apartment in the Cuffe Parade area some years back with their savings. It has a beautiful ocean view.'

Not really keen to know much more than I volunteered to inform her about my respectable background and parentage, she cut it short and asked me if I would like a cup of tea, in a tone that made me feel she hoped I would refuse her hospitality so that the meeting was of shorter duration than necessary, as Surya was not with us to sense her reserve with me.

'Tea would be fine, only if it's not a bother,' I replied.

The air was stiff! If she thought I was desperate to ingratiate myself, she was mistaken. I loved and wanted Surya for the rest of my life but not at any cost. At the price of mutual dignity, yes. But at any cost? No way! Staccato, one-line conversations ensued till the tea arrived, served up by a retinue of staff in uniforms, wearing safas, on a silver salver and a silver Cooke & Kelvey monogrammed tea set. The staff that carried the tea came as a welcome interlude to break the awkwardness both ways. My eyes wandered vacantly beyond the thick glass that looked on to palatial lawns with sprinkling waterbodies, as two peacocks strutted around while a bevy of maalis sat threading marigold malas, home-strung for the family's evening prayers, I was told.

At the far end of the 2-acre garden was Surya's covered swimming pool of some 5,000 square feet. I stared blankly as far as the eye could stretch. There was, beyond the pool, a vacant plot of land where Surya constructed a dwelling for us to live within the boundaries of the joint family, yet slightly secluded for a bit of privacy.

Just that once it was built, on instinct my mother had offered us, from the generosity of her heart, her ancestral home, just about a few minutes away from here, my preferred choice too. Though this was unconventional, it took a year to persuade Surya to alternate between the two homes and that he was not being put through an uncomfortable choice that could tear him away from his roots.

The meeting wasn't going as anticipated. Conversation was stifled, with long awkward stretches of deafening silence. 'Ma'am, are you fond of travelling?' I inquired, to which she said, 'No. I only frequent my Guru ji in Vrindavan...'

I struggled to hastily finish my hot cup of tea almost burning my lips, so I could say my 'shukriya', my thanks (but actually, no thank you!) for being so distant and unwelcoming, in order to dismiss myself from the intimidating environment. 'It was nice of you to spare some time to meet me. *Aapka bahut bahut dhanyawaad. Main chalti hoon*, as I have an important meeting.'

'Theek hai. Namastey...aap chaliye, phir. Aapke paas gaadi hai?'

'Jee haan. Main apni gaadi mein aayi hoon, thank you very much.'

Not much was said or spoken in those twenty minutes that seemed to last forever. That's just what hurt and humiliated me, as so little was said. And yet, a lot was palpable by my tender heart.

I fled with tears streaming down my cheeks, waiting for my driver to bring the car onto the porch. Out in the open air, to get into the warmth of my little Fiat car that was cosier and warmer than that cold house... to leave for my own aviary of mirth and laughter, truly my own little world, far, far away from Mrs Mittal's orbit.

~

My emotional takeaways after meeting Amma ji were sad and dewy. It was one of those dark nights of the soul. I couldn't ever confess to Surya how abrupt and distant his mother was after he had left us alone to get acquainted. I was left guessing what she must have said to him, when mother and son met again, about her impressions of me.

I fleetingly felt if this was to be my permanent abode, I would choke within the confines of this overpowering opulence, devoid of mirth or warmth, suffocated within its claustrophobic chambers, gagged to death without love or a whiff of oxygen to nurture my natural and playful emotions. My mind flitted to royal families one read of, replete with palace intrigues. This palace must have its fair share of power play too, I thought, in which I would be a complete misfit.

No! I had made up my mind that if this culminated in wedlock, I would have my own love nest in an act of early defiance to maintain my freedom. Suryaprakash would have to make his uncomfortable choices. I didn't belong to this set-up which was in sharp contrast to my middle-class home that resounded with loads of love and laughter and lesser wealth to squabble over.

I wasn't going to impinge on Surya's right to a joint family business or shake up the edifice of his home. Nor would I be scheming to fester a feud, but I could surely opt to maintain my dignity and respect to live separately.

I was to realize later that Amma ji was reluctant to really meet me, forget welcoming me. She had condescended only upon Surya's insistence in setting up this preliminary meeting as protocol, to acquaint her with the woman he intended to marry, to which she strategically yielded so as not to incur his defiance.

I was to experience, as years went by with Surya, that royalty, as also stiff-upper-lipped business aristocratic families and their scions, were reared in the most robotic manner to never express joy, mirth, grief, heady laughter or tears. It was a cardinal rule of adhering to a fake, stoic demeanour, never to wail at funerals or jump for joy if they were elated. A warm hug or a mild peck on the cheek as greeting was considered too forward and licentious, symbols of Western culture and public displays of affection. A 'namaste' was the prescribed protocol of greeting.

Were these highbrowed families devoid of normal human emotions, were they insulated from them, or were they just a morbid, staid genre of mankind!?

~

Two years went by but we were nowhere close to getting married, when Surya said to me, 'Akshraa, I need to win over my mother and gain her approval, so we need to defer our plans for an indefinite period. Would you agree to settle in France for a year or two till then? I will gift you the most luxurious mansion of your choice. Also, as I have business interests there, I will be around very often to be with you. Don't worry, you will not be alone. You can take an entourage of staff members to accompany you...' I was in utter shock when I heard this proposition! Was he striking a deal? Offering me an emotional bribe for indefinite procrastination? Inclined to do away with my presence? Somewhere within, I knew he was stalling. I sensed he was buying time in keeping his options wide open. I was beginning to feel a sense of his power over me by now, how being with a richer man meant that he firmly set the rules of the game. It was going to be his call all the way, and the only choice I could exercise was to close it right here.

'Akshraa, I don't mean to play with your emotions. Understand this: in business families like mine my family members are co-owners in industry and assets. If I oppose their wishes outright, someone within can insist on a formal split. Can I afford that just because my heart is set on you? You do understand, surely!'

'No, I don't understand. I really don't. Don't tell me you didn't know of these impediments as you and I went deeper into this relationship?'

'I did. But I don't know if I can afford to let go of my business interests for the sake of a woman…'

'A woman?' I yelled. 'Listen, you've said it all. I am not going to get into a slugfest with you on who comes first: your family, business, or me.' It was quite clear, I was the third priority. 'You, Mr Mittal, are a weakling. A wimp. Let's call it a day. I never want to see you again,' I ended.

Unfortunately I was too involved in the relationship to quit midway, partly because I shirked confronting another failed relationship. The situation was beginning to seem like an emotional tug-of-war too soon, an uneasy truce at best.

He patronizingly offered, 'I will come and meet your parents and convince them of my bonafides and of my sincere intent to marry you. It is just a matter of time before Amma agrees.'

I took it to Mom and Dad: 'Surya wants to call on you,' briefing them on what had transpired with his mother. I saw tears well up in my parents' eyes as Daddy managed to shake himself out of a quivering voice, turning stern as he cautioned me, 'Akshraa, my answer is firm. You never paid heed to my admonishing you in your younger years about marrying that Bengali. You are an adult and a mother today, and since you are not financially dependent on us, you probably feel you can ignore our plea. I don't care if he is a scion from the House of Mittals…I will not meet Mr Suryachandra or whatever is his name… Know this, Akshraa, you were too young and defiant when you decided to marry Arnaab against our wishes. This will be your second blunder. As much as we dissuaded you from marrying Arnaab because he was neither from our community nor from the same social strata, we hold the same yardstick regarding the Mittals. They are one of the richest families of India. You are the daughter of a proud bureaucrat who has lived his life on principles and inculcated the same in you. The middle class don't marry industrialists. It's a mismatch again. A blunder, should you again commit to this rishtaa. You will never be treated well by them...they will always look down and talk down to you. In our society, class and community matter. Never contemplate marrying a man below your status or above it. Don't ride on his riches, rather stand tall and achieve heights on your own merit. There are no shortcuts to life. A man like this will always keep you enslaved with his wealth. You will live a pampered life but have little power in exercising your choice of free will within their joint family.'

A sense of déjà vu struck. Dad's disapproval of Arnaab and his family not being good enough for his daughter had come back to haunt me, but this time the resistance came from the Mittals.

~

After Dad's stern speech, it dawned upon me that he made sense. I was levelling out.

I thought over the option Surya had offered me. He had put forward a fait accompli. I felt short-changed for the sincerity of my affections. Saddened, I quit seeing him. Firmly, my answer was a 'No' to his proposition of sending me away, and dispensing with me by consigning me to a lonely life in a 'prison without bars' within some imaginary castle. I stood my ground.

'Surya, I was born and brought up here. I own a grand roof over my head in Lutyens' Delhi, a coveted address, plus I have a reasonable income of my own as I have fortunately not yet quit my job. I could dispense with someone who is going to forcibly ordain the course of my life. I will live in the country of my birth and within my little palace in Golf Links.'

Down I was, but not out. I distanced myself from him, my

bourgeois pride rebutting any overtures from Suryaprakash.

On the verge of losing Love Game II, a sense of defeat had begun to engulf me, a feeling of deep rejection at being dispatched out of my country. I couldn't attach a label to this relationship; it was too amorphous to define. But endless dating with no commitment was not worth it. It was hardly an offer for marriage. Dad was right. Surya was enticing and entrapping me into a luxurious life and its perks in the hope I would comply with being probably one of the many damsels in his life.

ᔓ

We didn't meet. Formally, it was over.

The long break must have given him space and time to reflect. Maybe not. It didn't matter. But that same space and time made me turn my back on him, not as a game plan but actually to shut a rotten bargain. It was many months before he tried to revive a dying affection. His outreach towards me began with persistent moves at striking a conciliation to revive our relationship. By then I was cold. Hardened and indifferent to his moves, suspicious of his next ploy.

A lot of spontaneity and affection had waned by now, because I was coming of age, confronting an ugly truth in its naked light. What would or should a woman at this stage have done in an unequal situation?

ᔓ

As time went by, I immersed myself in my work once more. I had thought I would quit my job once we were married or take a sabbatical for a while. But I began to treat my job at HCL as a therapy once again, to drug and suppress my loneliness, seldom socializing in the evenings.

On a one-off outing when I went out at night with a group of friends to No. 1, a disco at Taj Mansingh, I glimpsed Surya sitting alone at the bar. I least expected that encounter, as I avoided frequenting his familiar habitats. I glanced at him from the corner of my eye. He didn't come my way either. Thankfully, I was spared any awkwardness. My heart skipped a few beats, but more than that, I felt disdain at seeing him at close quarters. After the first round of drinks, I requested my friends if we could shift the venue and head up to Casa Medici on the rooftop, as this was too close for comfort.

That night, my phone rang endlessly. I had no doubt who it was and refused to pick it up. The next morning I got a van full of red roses which had one solitary white rose in its midst, with a note that read, 'Aksh, you are that one in a million, like the white rose.' It should have done something to me! But I was numb. It stirred nothing within me. Those roses he sent as a tease would wilt and wither away over the next few days or however long was their lifespan. A woman doesn't bloom on tears, surely.

I let it pass. The gesture didn't warrant a response.

~

Two months later, he arrived unexpectedly around 7 in the evening. I was taken aback to see him at my doorstep, but feigned being distant yet maintained the etiquette of being correct and formal. 'Akshraa, we need to talk.'

'May I offer you a cup of coffee, Surya?' I hadn't forgotten my manners. I spoke in a measured, modulated tone, 'I don't really like to drink on weekdays, Surya. So how may I extend my hospitality to you as a visitor—tea, coffee or a nimbu pani?' My body language was consciously one of signalling to my visitor that I didn't want a prolonged evening.

'Akshraa, I really and truly want to marry you and have told my family that Akshraa is non-negotiable. If you are not supportive of my decision to marry her, she and me will have a quiet wedding out of town and I will move house with her.' I sensed I had now got him where I wanted him.

'Speak for yourself, Surya. That's your decision. I prefer to live alone, focus on my job, and devote my time to bringing up my son. What your empire means to you, my livelihood and my job is to me. Your decision to reopen this chapter doesn't validate nor negate me in any way. You or your family's opinion of me is not my reality.'

~

I behaved distant, but deep down, yearned to surrender and trust the process of life. 'I think I am being too hard on myself and harsh on him. Sitting on a high horse is stupid if true love beckons,' I told myself. Gradually I became responsive and believed Surya's sincere attempts at an outreach by just letting go of misunderstandings and dismissing them as his frailty in being torn between his attachment to his family and his love for me. While choosing a life partner, it is seldom a predictable and linear progression of emotions, as it's difficult to sometimes control the flow of circumstances. These were just hiccups before the final steps of any man and woman in the process of making up one's mind with who you want to spend the rest of your life with, I reasoned. The heart had its yearnings and family obligations their pulls, in the opposite directions.

Our Wedding in Mykonos: A Half-bride?

WE TOOK OUR first seven steps into marital bliss at Mykonos in Greece. Chartering a flight to celebrate with just about a hundred guests, we flew to the island for a three-day celebration as we wanted to keep it warm and intimate, preferring understated elegance to a band-baajaa-baaraat wedding in Delhi. The events planner had curated all the ceremonies within this exotic locale.

On the first night, young glamorous hostesses sporting Greek olive branch tiaras, dressed in white, greeted our guests at a quaint restaurant by the Aegean Sea.

The following day was a brunch party at the beach restaurant Nammos, amidst a setting of bright flowers, blue-and-white linen and royal silver drapes to blend with the azure skies and the turquoise waters of the sea. The afternoon sun was mild, tempting revellers to jump into the water for a swim, while the rest sang along to karaoke alternating between popular Bollywood and English numbers.

The marriage rituals took place to the sounds of mantras renting the air as live flautists played along when I entered the mandap, embellished with a sprinkling of Swarovski crystals which emitted a subtle sparkle, shimmering like stars against the night sky. '*Taare bhi zameen par*?' I smiled to myself, thanking

God for this never-ever moment.

It was a splendorous atmosphere for the big day with a lively palette of purples and pinks, crystal vases, candles and lanterns… to conjure a dreamy scene bustling with sparkle and romance. The floral compositions on the next day were striking, arrayed with bouquets of delicate peonies, roses and wild eryngiums as far as the eye could stretch.

There was laser lighting all around, as fireworks illuminated the night sky in the Island of Winds where sleep stopped being a necessity and became a luxury. The flowers used for the night of the wedding were again different from the first day with loads of gypsophila (baby's breath), white freesias and orchids dendrovium.

The entire setting felt like entering the kingdom of gods by this seaside location on Psarou beach.

Champagne on ice in silver holders with truffles and caviar did the rounds on trolleys. This venue had been the hang-out of soccer stars and shipping magnates who retired after sunset at the restaurant to indulge in freshly caught fish that was arrayed on ice, moonlighting the hours away.

~

Moonlight and merriment…

This was how it appeared to our guests. The hospitality, the glitz and glamour was nothing like it seemed! As I was getting dressed, slipping into my lehenga, Surya called my room, so the attendant who picked up the phone informed me of the urgency. 'Ma'am, Mr Mittal says he needs to talk to you right now.' I thought it was a sweet-nothing call to say I love you. 'Can you just tell him I am running twenty minutes late to get to the ceremony, as my hair's not done and my nail polish hasn't dried, so it will smudge if I attend to his call?'

'It's important. Please get her to speak to me as I hold the line.'

'Honey, bear with me,' I said. 'I will be there sooner than you know…to be knotted to you for the rest of my life. Just give me twenty minutes more…till I am with you forever and ever.'

'Akshraa. Stop right here. Let the festivities go on for our guests. They've come all this way to felicitate us. But we can't complete the ceremonial ritual of going around the fire. My family has got an inkling that we are out of India not on a vacation but to get married. My sister has just called to convey an ultimatum. Should we get formally married, the family wants a split in business… My Nana ji is threatening to go on a fast unto death should I marry you.'

Shocked. Diminished. Angry. Humiliated on my first night of marriage, I missed a few heartbeats. Drenched in profuse sweat, a medley of emotions ran through my chest as I shook myself out of this defeat to think with my head for now and deal with the stab on my heart later. 'Surya, I thought you told your family I am non-negotiable?!' As I uttered my words in a knee-jerk reaction, my self-preservation instincts took over. 'I'll make a deal with you… Let's go on with the rituals of the ceremony in the eyes of the public. I beg of you, please redeem my honour. Don't let me down in public view…once we return to India, we will live apart. You can always deny our marriage to your family…that we were just vacationing with a large group of friends.' I didn't want to give him much time to think and aimed at closing the deal. 'Deal!' I thought in my mind! Is marriage ever a deal? For me, it was. Subconsciously, from now on, my dignity was at stake. He had little or nothing to lose, while I had my honour to salvage.

Alas! I thought, would every step of my relationship entail a negotiation for the rest of my life? Did it leave any scope for the spontaneity of true love? The family had pulled the trigger from far away, a Damocles sword hanging on our head forever.

Had I unwittingly tied the knot to a puppet on a string? I had married one of the most eminent personages, a powerful man who was powerless when pitted against the might of his fraternity, a hostage to their commands. I felt small deep within me, knowing I had bartered my soul in exchange for the honour I craved, for the rest of my life. The night-of-dreams turned into a night-of-shame which only I knew, an experience that scarred me for life in the awareness that I was beholden to a man I could never depend on, and had to always think first of my own survival.

Was this a half-marriage? Was I a half-bride?

Life after Mykonos

WHEN WE RETURNED to India, Surya kept up the charade to appease his family, so we stayed in separate homes for a year. His family heard that we did get married in Mykonos but he denied it vehemently, saying these were just rumours or wouldn't he be staying with me? Even if they felt the logic was unconvincing, there's little they found to nail him. Surya took a year to acclimatize them to the reality of my existence in his life and to come to terms that even if there was no acceptance of me, the relationship was not something they could wish away.

Days rolled into months and months rolled into tearful years. We didn't quite live happily ever after but we did live together as man and wife. After the initial pinpricks, everything settled into a pattern, except that our families never met or crossed paths. Suryaprakash began to divide his time between two homes, his family residence and my house, but seldom did the twain meet. Tensions escalated a few times a year till the dust settled after each periodic emotional outburst. Having to reconcile to Surya living out of two homes was a painful process. I was as unyielding as his family was unaccepting. The conflicts never allowed me to settle into the comfort of complacency, feeling like an outcast and a pariah, living on the edge most of my life.

But Surya had become immune because he had started loving the parallel life, not needing to answer or explain where he was going or what he did with his time, rotating his existence between the two houses whose residents were too hostile to each other to ever compare notes. The inadvertent divide-and-rule, though not of Surya's doing, worked to his advantage. If a situation that he didn't want to deal with presented itself in either home, the threat loomed large that he would absent himself, being unavailable and inaccessible for days on end. I didn't have the wherewithal to keep stalking or tracking daily movements. In any case, who in their right mind would even be curious to want to track any human being's moves 24x7!

The only time his family and me met was for the evening puja on Dhanteras, choti Diwaali and Diwaali, where Surya had made it clear to the family he would be bringing me along and refused to perform the rituals alone. They conceded grudgingly. They didn't want to antagonize Surya to the extent that he would completely stop frequenting them, while I was equally insecure to rock the boat or throw ultimatums. Over the years, the vibes remained cold and distant with his family members. They were not rude but turned mildly accepting of me partaking of the family rituals and an occasional meal together, once or twice a year. Greetings started with a 'pranaam' at Amma ji's feet and farewells were the same. However, his two younger sisters, Karuna and Chitra, were very loving and supportive. Both of them were happily married and lived in Delhi.

~

As years went by, deep down, more than anything, I craved to win Surya's respect by proving I wasn't this airhead who only enjoyed the high life. I had skills of my own which lay in abeyance, which I wanted to optimize in order to fulfil my creative potential and use my time productively, by adding value to his empire, instead of living in the shadow of just being a rich man's wife. What better way was there to win a man's heart? Wasn't any accomplished woman sexier if she had brains too?

Having had an earlier understanding and experience of the business world, I loved the play. I yearned for a fuller expression of my potential to recreate the years in HCL, where I made my initial fortune, when I knew no fear of how to get there—where not to succeed was not an option...with no 'Plan B' in sight. Perhaps with just possessing the arrogance of youth in those days, which came with a knowing certitude that the business world was just a playground, and the only virtue needed to succeed was to remain 'paranoid'!

What better way was there to win my husband's heart and respect than to prove that I had an ignited mind, instead of remaining a homemaker on the sidelines, or learning culinary skills in cordon bleu cooking?

But alas! I felt discriminated from the other family members in not being given a platform to work within their business, as Surya was too mild to assert my inclusion in the joint family set-up. I felt belittled, unworthy and small. At the age of fifty I hardly wanted to get a master to teach me classical singing or dancing, or skill me in the arts of soft culture, when my spirit was yearning to take wing in a flight of cerebral fantasy. I wanted so much to take off from where I had left off twenty years back, to reinvent and relearn the world of business in a new India. So much had changed in the world of business. I yearned to relearn and get back to it all.

Feeling excluded from working within the comfort zone of the family chain became a bone of contention between me and Surya, leading to bickering and frequent feuds. Most business families did not approve of working women. In the eyes of the world I had it all, but deep down, I knew I was staring at a void. I was hardly looking to become a millionaire on my own steam, nor had notions of being some genius. All I wanted was to get back to work, to challenge the stagnation and status quo of the still and idle life I had been leading for years.

I felt slighted as Surya sided with family members in denying me my need to optimize my skills to their fuller potential. Every tiff became an acrimonious 'me vs them'. Long silences and frequent verbal duels drove the wedge wider as tensions escalated to bitter chasms. It made me feel as if after so many years of being married, I never really belonged, till the harshest words spoken to me hit like a sledgehammer: 'Akshraa, I made a mistake in marrying you; you are sounding like a pain. If it's a choice between my family and you, know for sure that they come first. I care for you enough not to sever our bond, but I cannot afford a family split on account of your demands. Just get off my back, will you? I have never denied you the privileges of money. Go buy what you like, go on an exotic vacation, but working within the business is a firm no!'

This was turning into a battle of nerves. 'So what do I do with my time?' I yelled. 'You said you disapprove of idle socializing. I agreed. Now do you just want me to read and become a closet scholar? Learn Bharatnatyam? Go to an art class? Join an organization of ladies who are into charity? Frankly, none of these options interest me. Go take up a job at the age of fifty with a multinational company, when I haven't worked in so many years? At least if I could work for and within the family fold, I can get your guidance, while simultaneously do an online refresher course to keep abreast with the latest in the business world, Surya!'

I remembered the thrill I had experienced while splurging

from my own earnings years back. It was so rewarding to indulge in pleasures occasionally with my self-earned money, as it gave me a sense of self-worth and self-pride. I would have loved to buy my husband a Patek Philippe watch on his birthday with my own earnings instead of gifting him something from the monthly stipend he generously gave me. It was a secret thrill that I would have loved to surprise him with, just to see a smile on his face and get a warm hug in return.

I felt deeply rejected, empty and hollow. Doing nothing other than sitting at home day in and day out or partying the night away was depressing. It made me feel so wasted—where did nearly a decade of my life go if, despite my loving devotion to Surya and building my world around him, I actually had no world left?

After years of marriage, I felt like an outsider, and rationally or irrationally, I took it to heart as an inference of a lack of support from my man who should have wanted to nurture my creative needs. Imposed domesticity, voluntary or compulsory, was most women's dilemma—how to fill a void once children had grown up and had a life of their own. The 'empty nest syndrome' then began to gnaw, as the soul strived for expression of a fuller entity, as marriage after so many years wasn't just about property and propriety, but togetherness and being apart, that vital space that allows two people to also grow in emotion and intellect.

∾

Reflections thereafter

My reflections alternated between pride and despair thereafter. Albeit, my circumstances were specific; I don't generalize. But most middle-aged women had difficulty in reinventing a distinct identity for themselves either out of complacency or limitations from within the family. In a changing India, women were loath to surrender anymore to conservative authority or antiquated elders demanding subservience to male dominance. I was no different.

While women were asserting their constitutional rights more fiercely than ever before, a yawning gap existed in their knowledge of how to empower themselves financially or find ways to give a fuller expression of aptitude and free themselves from male feudalism. Surely, there had to be a niche even at this age for me to reinvent myself if I wanted to live a more fulfilling life.

Regardless of my specific predicament, I widened this thought to ponder upon what kind of India we had imagined for our women. I used to have frequent and intimate chats with my peers, few who were fortunate to possess talent and were encouraged by their spouses. But that was an exception. An ambitious woman who dreamt big was most men's nightmare. Women with education plus money equalled power, which were the two intimidating and uncomfortable ideas in a male dominated society that threatened its very foundations. Why? Because the idea of an empowered woman earning a living was seldom encouraged, as it threatened the very concept of family life, to which she was the caregiver. Owning financial resources that would have come from the woman of the house's earnings would have been a scarier thought, highly intimidating to the male ego. Aside from women's liberation, which comprised just ideational campaigns, this was a REAL threat, not a perceived one.

Though India had opened up to a free-market economy over two decades back, the moral codes for dressing, drinking, dating or working still adhered to the last century. How was this in sync with a free world then? A free-market economy necessitated not just a free flow of trade but also an ideational evolution of thoughts in reshaping traditional notions of gender. For example, though Surya admired working women, he was reluctant to allow me that domain, albeit in my case, due to his own meekness in combating his family's reservations.

I lived a privileged life within the confines of opulence, protected and cordoned from the world of reality, a lot like the princesses of Arab countries, whose outer world was magnificent, yet their inner world was devoid of fulfilment. It became stifling at most times; despite the plenitude that surrounded me, I felt confined, repressed, and loveless, a goldfish in a Baccarat bowl.

I found that most women who were at midlife, and were educated and belonged to the elite strata, took to playing cards, golf, kitty parties or to religion to fill a void at that stage of life, completely dependent on their spouses financially, as also too afraid to stand up for themselves, forget stand up and claim their property rights over male members of the family: brothers or spouses. 'Disguised slavery' as Chetan Bhagat called it?

Whatever their joy or route to salvation—kitty parties, higher cerebral pursuits or spiritual evolution—no one was anyone to judge which was the best way to transit from middle age to old age. Just that one could die of dementia or loneliness if one didn't have a productive pastime by this phase of life, and turn a parasite preying off others for company, affections or financial security. I wasn't the kind of mother who demanded excessive face-time with my children beyond the minimum graces of civility and reverence, as these were prime years for them to build a strong edifice for themselves and the next generation.

I had observed amongst my peers that women even in affluent households didn't have a say on where to deploy finances in a patriarchal system, this being the norm rather than an exception. Neither were they the decision-makers of family savings even in middle-class homes. Their level of financial literacy was just inadequate to non-existent, whether through choice, ignorance or per force.

As the thoughts I penned in my diary progressed, I felt I wanted to give a larger message to womankind, something that propelled the momentum of my script, and that was to rebuild in women a trust in one's own prowess and in the incredible powers that each of us is gifted with, forgotten somewhere and buried in the depth of their being. Once that power was ignited and realized financially and emotionally, we as humans were not slaves to affection or based our sense of self-worth conferred by the success of man-woman relationships. A man-woman relationship then became a part of a whole, not one's entire universe.

There were rich, reasonably educated and yet depressed and lonely housewives in India who lived fatigued domestic lives catering to the needs of husbands and children, socializing as the only pastime, having ignored their own development.

I yearned to reach out and implore them, 'Build a parallel universe, more gratifying to the inner self, and stand up for yourself. I am all what I am...and much more!'

Part III

The Heady Highs of Lutyens' Living: Life and Times with Surya

The Dark Side of Desire in Lutyens'

THE LUTYENS' WORLD, for the uninitiated, was and still remains a heritage area in the capital of India, named after the British architect Edwin Lutyens who was responsible for much of the architectural design and building when India was part of the British Empire in the 1920s. 'God's little acres' housed the highest-ranking officials of the country, from the President and the Prime Minister spiralling downwards to the 'Delhi Durbar', which comprised the hallowed and impenetrable circle of the PM's Cabinet colleagues, bureaucrats, Chief Justices, the military brass and some of India's wealthiest business houses. This habitat was and still is considered one of the most expensive districts in the world, spanning under a thousand homes privately owned, where the snobbery and prejudice of residing close to this acropolis defined social status.

In a sense it's a zone inhabited by near-aliens who do things differently. They think, dress and behave as polar opposites to any other affluent city in the world. Its lush and expansive boulevards soak in its exclusivism as much as its cosmopolitanism. People residing here are mostly a self-obsessed, selfie breed, considering themselves exotic avians who roam within this surreal periphery. I was self-enslaved within this suffocatingly splendid world, trapped within its illusions. Loving it and hating it, having become a compulsive addict to its life and lifestyle.

There existed a world of secret and surreptitious lives tucked away within the secret paradise of Lutyens' Delhi. As you drove down its wide roads lined with majestic Ashoka trees, amidst low-rise bungalows, sprawling manicured lawns and verdant foliage that formed the topography of this international city, entry within its formidable gates and hallowed circles was strictly by invitation, gatecrashers being frowned upon as pariah.

Closeted within these confines were dirty secrets and dark desires of use and abuse that formed the ugly underbelly of a glamorous life. The Lutyensites spoke a different language and dressed in a macabre way as their social mannerisms bordered on the unpredictable-eccentric. Living in Lutyens' was like life on another planet, the likes of which were hard to encounter in even the most prosperous metropolises of the world.

Hedonistic revelry within this milieu was a cult in a country where two square meals were a luxury, electricity a rarity and basic clothing a bigger luxury.

The rich in India, a sizeable clan, were as discerning and rarefied as the air they breathed, the spirits they consumed or the estates they owned. A motley charade of Halloween played out round the year, in dress as well as in mannerisms. I am prone to sounding a trifle apologetic of the conspicuous consumption in retrospect, as sadly, we did live in a country of vast economic disparity.

You could almost pigeonhole the party lot into the likes of migratory birds who aired themselves, mostly at nocturnal hours. Some slept by day, waking to dress up for evening revelry, an orgy of parties, 'shots' and 'snorts' to burn the midnight hour, while the rest of India burned the midnight oil in toil.

Between the have and have-nots was a clear divide as sharp as black and white, with no shades of grey, something that had the power to set me on a pensive journey of post-revelry remorse, to re-evaluate my worldview and critique my newly donned sensibilities or a trifling and sinful lack of sensitivity.

A herdish infra culture was the 'Berkin-Brigade', society bimbettes who strove hard for one second of visibility in a Page 3 photo op.

There were three species that comprised this motley universe of the lunching ladies: the PYTs, the middle-aged divas, and the auntie jis. They lived to network and flaunt a privileged and vacuous life.

'Auntie mat kaho,' was the prototype of an ageing woman refusing to come to a graceful acceptance of life's progression, sporting a Hello Kitty bag, some dyed blonde in their fifties, looking like Barbies-gone-wrong. It's admirable in a way, as she wanted to retain a contemporary and zesty mindset, believing the sixties were the new forties. Most at middle age were so botoxed that it was hard to detect facial expressions of delight or anger, as one felt that frown lines reflected etchings of character and a life well lived. But with silicon implants between the furrows, it was difficult to guess the mood.

I was tickled pink when I eavesdropped on a new party game of the affluent: guessing the latest to have entered the botox circuit, gauging from how Mongolian someone looked. 'Did you see Manjula recently? She looks like a chimp. I think she will have to wait till her botulin wears off to get a better job done next time! The upward slant in her brows makes her look like Cruella de Ville, the antagonist of *101 Dalmations*, stern and severe...' Injections and infusions, the rich felt, could buy age too, even if it meant going in for vampire facials to reverse ageing.

Delhi suffered from a severe dysfunctional disorder of OTT

(over-the-top) dressing and desires. A city of shopping addicts, the Punjabi kudi loved everything loud, from platinum blonde Goldilocks streaks, to auburn tints, to the beat of Yo Yo Honey Singh's pelvic gyrating music, to Swarovski bags, diamanté shoes, shimmery nail colours, even couture diamanté lingerie. If they just bought a monogrammed Gucci/LV/Prada/Chanel clutch, fake or real, it warranted a selfie that was instantly flashed online on their BlackBerry Messenger, Twitter, Facebook profiles. This 'I have to have it' fixation started from ten-year-old kids wanting to wear a T-shirt printed with 'My dad is an ATM', who grew into women feeling 'My husband's my ATM'. Attitude was on the footpaths, on the streets, in their cars, in the air…

I never understood the desperation of social butterflies striving to achieve visibility in glossies. I personally regretted idling away those productive years, when I should have aspired towards celebrity-hood by appearing on Page 1 of leading dailies and be in Indra Nooyi's (of Pepsi fame) brains or Facebook COO Sheryl Sandberg's shoes, to be known for my acumen at excelling in a particular domain instead of wasting energies on social photo ops.

The rat race amongst the glitterati came as comic relief, if you could just view it as a bystander. But the trouble with being in the rat race was that at the end of it, you remained just that: a rat! I've eavesdropped on a conversation that went something like this, 'Babes, she hosted a swanky party, with the entire media at her calling. Considering she is my best friend, look what she did to me! When I saw the pictures five days later in a tabloid, she had released shots of me taken from my worst angle, just to put me down. To make it worse they were miniscule pictures of me since she wanted the centre spread for herself. In future, I will never show up at her dos like some filler.' (*Sulk!*)

If I sound like a muckraker for deriding her complexes, do forgive me my trespasses. All is fair in love and war. And all was fair in playing careless whispers within the Lutyens' circle.

High Points of the High Life

ANY REASONABLY HAPPY marriage has its fair share of love, laughter and squabbles. Ours was no different. We enjoyed the good life, a modicum of socializing and the intimacy of doing things together often. It was like any other marriage. There were good days, fun-filled days and rotten days. Mundane and boring times, followed by unexpected impromptu and thrilling moments. As years rolled by, I felt our bonds strengthen.

We were much in love; there was nothing that a sweet 'sorry' could not resolve.

In the land of plenty: Switzerland

The years we were together, an annual getaway to the paradise of Switzerland, the land of lush landscapes and slush monies, was habitual. To renew over a family vacation in the verdant playground of the rich and famous, the undulating greens of Gstaad, experience fine dining in the plush environs of the Jungfrau hotel at Interlaken, or simply moonlighting down Lake Geneve with the crisp Alpine air caressing your face, was routine. Surya, by himself, had seen enough of the high life. Deep down he was modest, a simpleton who would never fuss or throw attitude with people from any walk of life. But he did love pampering me to a fault.

The formal dress codes in Interlaken over dinner was a solitaire on your finger and perhaps a Patek Philippe watch on the wrist. Bejewelled and bewitched, the seriously wealthy spent time chatting over candlelight dinners with classic lounge melodies playing unobtrusively in the background, while one probably lunched with a con-artist banker in Zurich out to entice you into laying his slimy hands on your corpus to park it in Sleazeland. It was a normal occurrence to come across the Mumbai-Delhi business circles in a huddle with bankers years before the advent of Internet made face-to-face meetings unnecessary, easing the speed and convenience with which capital travelled freely and virtually across borders. If ever it could be said about a nation, 'A country where money never sleeps,' it would be Switzerland, going by the sheer nature of what it sold to the world at large—the secrecy of parking illicit fortunes in this safe haven.

I was informed humorously that no one was indiscreet in acknowledging a chance encounter with a friend that the suited-booted 'gora' banker he supped with was really from a Swiss financial institution. If one chanced on meeting a known friend, the introduction would be, 'Do meet a business associate...' Surya and I laughed at the charade that played out, as I was wonderstruck with the games of the rich and famous that descended on Swiss shores for laundering illicit wealth. However, these were only stories, as no one could point a finger at anyone, as Swiss secrecy laws protected and perpetuated the system.

Stretched limos with French-speaking chauffeurs drove us to the opulent casinos of Devon. Time was serious money as you sipped your Saint Julian Ducru-Beaucaillou in long-stemmed flutes while gambling at the casino. On the neighbouring table one could have sighted an international sports or film star, a mandarin of industry or a wily Russian czar dining at the restaurant that adjoined the gambling area.

At the end of the day, my thoughts reverberated to Oscar Wilde's exclamation, 'Dear Lord, give me the luxuries of life...I'll dispense with the necessities.'

~

Ayodhya and a game of poker

Indian Neros fiddled, like the fabled emperor, playing poker as Ayodhya burned. I don't write this with any sense of irreverence or superciliousness but what happened was an unintended and unplanned coincidence. The day's happenings were strange: a dizzying game of cards was being played at our home while a medieval monument fell like a pack of cards the same day, 6 December 1992.

The three domes of Babri Masjid were reduced to rubble by infuriated mobs with rods and stones. What began as 'kar seva' acquired a militant mood as fanatics hijacked the voice of reason, believing in their self-righteous cause. Zealots became the new messiahs of Hindu revivalism to undo historic injustices.

Some days are eerily extraordinary and this was one of those days. A week before, a game of poker had been planned at home, and being a masculine kind of sport, I was merely overseeing the cuisine and comfort of my guests as I chanced on a Breaking News story on BBC that was beaming on my screen in the bedroom.

I froze in shock and awe, glued to witnessing a sea of trishuls on the screen, as a frenzied multitude of sadhus turned militant, gripped by religious fervour to resurrect the rights of a repressed Hindu community. They took it upon themselves to undo the injustices of historic usurpation by Mughal invaders, to annex and reclaim Lord Rama's sanctum, his birthplace, hoping to rebuild the holy shrine by demolishing the mosque that stood in its place. It snowballed into an orgy of communal riots that revolted every voyeuristic viewer.

I watched the horror unfold, curled inside my blanket in the privacy of my bedroom. In the adjoining study room, the men's-only stag game was on in full swing. Being a polite hostess, I only made a brief appearance to say 'hello' to Surya's friends and make sure they were being attended to. There was a minister, a leading hotelier, a legendary cricketer of yesteryear and an industrial magnate playing for such high stakes that sent shivers down my spine as I witnessed the goings-on. Quite honestly, I was not even noticed and hardly acknowledged by any of my guests who were immersed in the game.

Luckily, Surya was only a host, having politely extricated himself from playing with this august group once they upped the stakes, though he did sportingly play a few rounds. He never ever gambled for such wondrous, obscene stakes. The amounts were so vulgar that the negotiation between the winner and loser was: which company should he sell to honour his losses or pay via a Cayman Island account? I heard this with my own ears, never having seen or known a world of such mad money. This was a predator's sport, one that only big boys with big bucks play at night.

The game with serious cash being burned was juxtaposed, though a total coincidence, with the annihilation of a religious shrine miles away from the capital. Both destructive! It was not as though we, as true patriots, were expected to go into instant national mourning unnaturally! It was like any normal day in Delhi, except that curfew had been imposed in some sensitive areas in Uttar Pradesh. The macabre events that played out that day felt weird.

I secretly wished I could have been a fly on the wall to hear live what was being transacted on the card table and experience the chills of gambling, yet I couldn't take my eyes off the melee on the television screen.

The hotelier, however, won a kingdom, a near-ransom, off the steel baron, an issue that never got sorted out and turned into an ugly spat of viciousness over the weeks to come. The latter had no intention to honour his losses. Gambling being an illicit pleasure, it was an equally illicit pact that had to be honoured in a contractual, unwritten code of ethics.

Now both the hotelier and the czar were coincidentally, unofficially and equidistantly close to the seats of power. Delhi got buzzing about the goings-on. Eventually, I heard, mediation at the highest levels settled the matter.

The closed-door manoeuvring of the rich and famous! Shatranj, a game of thrones, was in motion, as Midas was an unpredictable god in choosing whom he kissed and favoured!

What Surya lost to Bunny, the cricketer, before he quit the high-stakes game was paltry, hardly a sum fit for a queen's ransom, but enough for Bunny to gift his glamorous twiggy wife Romilla a stunning bracelet that she flaunted the next time we met. 'Boo,' she proceeded to tease me, 'I've got Surya Mittal wrapped around my wrist.'

I meowed back, 'Enjoy the moment, honey, because the next time the boys have a game, I hope to have Bunny around my finger...he may not win enough to get me a solitaire, but even a trinket would do to get even.' I smiled.

I sulked about this to Surya, who indulgently fluffed my hair and cajoled me, 'Bachiyaa, come on now, be a sport and let it ride.'

'Hmm! I guess you've never been lucky on the cards table, since you are lucky in love, as the cliché goes,' I retorted.

❧

Davos, January 2010

If it's January, it must be Davos!

It was a power and style statement to be seen around there, as the biggest names in the worlds of business, politics, policymaking and economics, be it George Soros, Bill Gates, Christine Lagarde or Joseph Stieglitz, participated in this networked extravaganza.

The sheer presence of movers and shakers congregating at one place made it a dream spectacle to be present at, with exposure to brilliant conversations between futurists, policymakers and business tycoons.

I implored Surya one winter, 'Can't you please participate in the Davos summit this year?' He disarmed me with his modesty and said, 'Aksh, I promise you, my love, give me just a few years to speed up my run-rate in my business. I may be doing reasonably well by Indian standards but not by the global parameters! It's the kind of event you don't arrive at if you are a virtual nobody in power or money. To be seated amongst the backbenchers of this august gathering would be a shame.' It was his way of initiating me into knowing there existed a hierarchy of layers even amongst the uber rich, the super-rich and the plain vanilla rich. In such a world, he must have deemed we stood way below the pecking order. However, many years later, I did get to accompany Surya to Davos for the summit.

I had watched international TV channels some years back, showing participants talking about problems in Europe, the growth of emerging markets and the challenge of climate change at Davos. But nothing prepared me for the pageantry I experienced in real life. Surya told me an annual membership to the WEF cost around $52,000, ticket and stay excluded. And to participate in the private industry sessions, which everyone agreed was where the real value was, you had to become an 'Industry Associate', which cost $1,37,000 a year. The dingiest of hotel rooms was $500 a night, while a private chalet was $1,40,000 for the week.

'So why did they all do it?' I asked.

As an example, the CEO of a major multinational explained to me that he and a colleague had meetings lined up with some thirty-six clients in the next three days. Their company sponsored the conference because aside from the branding, 'There's nowhere else in the world that they could get so many high-level meets into so little time, within one little village... Just board a flight and meet with the CEOs of dozens of global companies that buy millions of dollars' worth of your products and services every year.'

Parties, which were either large gatherings in the luxury Steigenberger Grandhotel Belvédère where we stayed or small get-togethers in a chalet, provided a setting for top executives to discuss transactions or other issues informally. Typically, the principals then consummated agreements in more informal settings. The founder of Facebook, Mark Zuckerberg, is rumoured to have gotten to know Sheryl Sandberg at the World Economic Forum in 2008, before offering her the post of Chief Operating Officer, as it was all about networking within this milieu.

Almost anyone who brushed by you was somebody of stature in the world. It could be an Ivy League economist, a decorated academician, a Russian mining czar, a Bollywood actor or the crown princess of Norway. I passed by Michael Dell of Dell in the corridors of the Steigenberger Grandhotel Belvédère one morning, as also caught a glimpse of Bill Gates strolling down the Promenade like any normal person, which was jam-packed with delegates, quite awestruck to see how they did things that commoners did too.

There were private fondue parties, a 'nightcap' bash thrown by a German media company and an after-dinner soiree at a Russian czar's chalet. WEF, I heard, put on half a dozen consolation events each night for the hapless guests who didn't get invited to any of these, like China's Dalian province sponsoring a buffet dinner at the Congress Centre.

I asked someone who was this 'Sorkin' everyone was buzzing about? Of course, Sorkin turned out to be the author of the international bestseller of the year, *Too Big to Fail,* and quite possibly the first one invited to every party in Davos, as he was considered the last word on economics. When one authored the inside story of how Wall Street and Washington fought to save the financial system and salvage themselves from the brink, his prophecies were perceived as coming from the Oracle!

~

As a first-time Davos attendee of a spouse, nothing had prepared me for the mix of awe and bewilderment I experienced. Over just four days, you got to break bread and rub shoulders with people who run our banks, charities and governments, and policymakers.

As a delegate said to me, 'Regulars who have been coming to Davos since a decade acknowledged that a lot of participants rarely spent much time inside the Davos Congress Centre, where world leaders delivered lengthy and boring speeches. The burning question at the Conclave by the evening was not the urgency of economic recovery or global warming but how to wrangle an invitation to Marissa Mayer's Yahoo party, or whether it was true that Mary J. Blige would sing at the Google bash.'

The following morning, I inquired from one of the delegates what the topic of discourse for the day's session at the Congress Centre was. 'Inequality,' he answered, in a very matter-of-fact way. 'They're talking about it in the cigar lounges, in the champagne pavilions, in the cocaine-atoriums.' Again, I was getting the drift…that when the world's richest people, who owned wealth equivalent to the poorest 3.5 billion, convened in this ski village of Switzerland, descending in their private jets to chart out the course of world economics, being served meals prepared by Michelin-starred London chefs, it made a mockery of philanthropy or the inequities of global distress they had gathered to resolve.

I had heard of the Google party, the McKinsey party, a ski party, a JP Morgan party or the Russian oligarch Deripaska's chalet do, a funky party where stuffed animals emitted laser beams from their eyes. Those with networking on their minds spent a lot of time at these events, until the wee hours, as it was night time in Davos when the real 'schmoozing' began, where cosying up to who you wanted to cultivate and striking up a conversation with people you've never met before was easy and informal.

In humility, I thanked God that if it was not for Surya, I would never have been exposed to this phantasmagoric spectacle, a truly once-in-a-lifetime opportunity.

We joined a group of oenophiles who comprised The Wine Forum, who had gathered over a hundred people swamping around the Piano Bar in the Hotel Europe, savouring Château Cheval Blanc and Château d'Yquem. By night, temperatures had dropped to -10°Celsius, as was forecast, so one was clad in serious winter gear, downing a glass of glutwein, a local speciality, just to feel a bit snug.

We were one of the many who were invited to Hubert Burda's soiree on the first night, a billionaire German publisher who had been sponsoring a party on the opening night of the forum for twenty-five years. I did catch a peek of the likes of Ms Mayer of Yahoo, talked briefly with the owner of one of Hong Kong's richest investment groups, and got a glimpse of a few top executives of some of the most renowned German companies like Deutsche Bank and Lufthansa.

❧

At midday, as I was sitting at a remote corner of the club lounge in the hotel perusing the morning papers, I observed that one could classify the club loungers from their dress, style and manners, identifying a business tycoon from a government policymaker or a banker. There was an eclectic buzz in the lounge with people chatting in Japanese, Chinese, French and German. A fairly young-looking man in his forties asked if he could be seated on the sofa next to me as the restaurant had filled up. He was furiously tapping on his phone, looking like he was closing in on a negotiation as he paced up and down till his battery ran out. The plug points were behind my sofa so he decided to recharge his smartphone, introduced himself to me, requesting if he could be seated on the opposite sofa and initiated a conversation to kill time. He was an Indian and my guess was right, he was a banker. 'I am Zaheer Khanna, CEO of Credit Suisse based in Delhi. Are you one of the delegates, ma'am?' he queried.

I smiled and extended my hand, 'I am Akshraa Mittal, also from Delhi. No, I am not a delegate but am here with my husband

Surya to witness the hoi polloi at this great economic fest.'

We then settled into an informal chat over coffee, after exchanging pleasantries.

'Are you involved with your husband's business too? If I recall, Mr Mittal is one of the prime players in the cement business, a very famous name and I read he's got a near monopoly on it, right?'

I smiled demurely and said, 'Yes, Mr Khanna, your information as a banker is bang on. No, I am not involved in a formal way with the business, though as a housewife I do chirp in with my impulsive instincts when asked. As for myself, I do track the financial world as I manage my own corpus. It keeps me wired. Tell me, Mr Khanna, what's your take on economic recovery post-2008?'

'Every now and then, the bogey of Fed tapering spooks the markets and jolts economic recovery, Mrs Mittal. Nouriel Roubini, in case you have not heard of him, the famous economist who foresaw the collapse of the U.S. housing market at that time, feels the rebound is a dangerous mirage as the Fed has made capital so cheap. The underlying disease is only suppressed. The recession is over but the crisis continues, according to the prophecy by this professor of doom and gloom,' he answered.

I concurred, 'I think people are losing faith in their national leaders the world over in combating public finances, unemployment, bank insolvencies or rising inflation. This crisis has eluded a solution to ever getting back to the boom times of pre-2008, despite the best global financial leaders' collective search for solutions. So, Mr Khanna, you are convinced the feel-good factor may elude us for yet another few years, as hopes of salvaging a lost decade seem a remote fantasy as of now?'

He proceeded to give me a deeper and more dangerous

interpretation about what he felt the future held. 'How many people think that in our lifetime we will never see another downturn like the one triggered by the Lehmann Brothers, despite the optimistic forecasts that economists give?'

'Gloomy,' I answered. Economic analysts were speculating whether the next lurking threat to global recovery would be a sinister terror attack by ISIS, an irrational Donald Trump becoming the US President or China's slowdown.

We spoke in passing about life in Delhi and exchanged mobile numbers.

Just then he heard a ring, yanked out his mobile from the plug and abruptly departed, 'Oops! That's my phone, Mrs Mittal. I was waiting for this call. Do excuse me. I hope you enjoy your stay here and let's catch up someday when back in Delhi. It was nice chatting with you. I didn't think laid-back homemakers like you knew much about the financial world. It was a refreshing change. All the best.'

❧

Fighting a Rajya Sabha election from Andhra Pradesh in 1995

Surya was contesting for a second term for a Rajya Sabha seat from Andhra Pradesh. So I wanted to tag along for a few days, just to be with him and see what being elected to the Upper House was all about. He was a nationalist and patriot to the core, extremely committed towards the causes he stood for, so I often went to watch him speak in Parliament during the nine years he was an MP. The party had nominated him twice over for being a loyalist, and had funded the elections big time the second time over.

In order to lobby hard with the local MLAs, we resided at the presidential suite of one of the city palaces of Hyderabad, with many adjoining rooms to organize one-on-one negotiations with herds of local kingpins to garner their votes. A handsome sum per legislator was apportioned by the local political party that gave Surya's opponent the ticket, for securing their mandate.

Middle class as I was, I was riveted like Alice in Wonderland about what all I could do with this princely ransom if I was one of those MLAs, my imagination running riot.

I spent most of those days reading under the balmy shade of trees in the Palace garden, going for a swim or peeking into the arcadia within the heritage hotel that was lined with jewellery stores and silverware crafted by local artisans. My heart was set on an emerald armlet worth a pittance in comparison to the funds for the election. I fantasized about owning it and sleeping with it that very night. I called up my soulmate Meera in Delhi and said, 'Meeru, there's this stunning piece I loved at the jewellers. But I am feeling awfully guilty about telling Surya that I want to pick it up and own it NOW!'

'Akshu! Uff. Don't be such a pleb. What's the big deal? The price of the bauble is paltry, like buying off a few votes. Don't fret the small stuff. Just go pick it up.'

Meera and I laughed off her quip like schoolgirls. It remained just that, a chuckle between two friends and a passing fantasy. The princess-of-nowhere, yours truly, was enthralled at Meeru's logic, chocolate to my ears…

But what of our legislators, most of whom were up for sale? Election season was the most lucrative time for horse-trading, especially in the event of a fractured mandate, for striking bargains in selling themselves to the highest bidder (discounts allowed, as in any commodity trading for numbers guaranteed.)

Passing a specific legislation or striking coalition deals were only two methods to amass wealth for MLAs, though their main profits and income came from the 'business of poverty' round the year. They behaved like local thugs on the prowl in their venality, pilfering from funds allotted towards floods, disasters, or MNREGA wages which were schemes meant for the jobless, or even stooping so low as making money off kidnappings. Perhaps only in a few Third World countries would scavenging off human misery be witnessed on such mass scale. It's sad! And We the People voted for them, but when the 'nation wanted to know' where their taxes went, there was no accountability, duped and damned to live with their heist till the next election season.

~

Changing personal and historical perspectives with the times

Surya, in the initial flush of romance, was slightly more patient and indulgent with me before the years rolled by and boredom and indifference set in. He cared to listen and agreed to disagree, or explain patiently to me, before he bordered on the contemptuous, especially on matters pertaining to Hindu 'garv', like rebuilding the Ram Mandir or his stance towards minorities.

'Aksh, you were born to a free India. I wasn't. You were educated in a convent. I studied in a public school where prayers were recited in Hindi. My grandfather was part of the freedom struggle...a friend of the founding fathers of the nation. Your grandfather was a Rai, Bahadur, a designation conferred on lackeys of the Raj, without meaning to sound offensive to you or wanting to belittle your family, that's the truth.'

'So?'

'So nothing. Yet everything. The truth of India's history as you studied it was obscured by "Macaulay putras". Today you are reading about the ideological war that rages between "Macaulay putras" and "dharti putras". The real heroes of the freedom struggle were Bhagat Singh, Netaji Subhas Chandra Bose and Sardar Patel, who were relegated in prominence due to a deliberate suppression of historic facts and the collective amnesia of the past regime. They are only now being posthumously accorded their due eminence. Courtesy the Nehru-Gandhi dynasty having ruled since Independence, barring thirteen years of intermittent reign by other coalitions, much was obfuscated during their time. I should know, as when I was a kid, Sardar Patel and Jinnah frequented my grandfather. Our ancestral home was the hang-out for frequent political parleys. I would get to hear excerpts from Amma when family discussions took place, though I couldn't make much of them, being so young myself.'

'Surya, I can only believe what I read in my history books in Loreto Convent. How can I imagine we were never taught authentic history? Even Nehru's amour with Lady Mountbatten was never out in the open in those years. It only came tumbling out of the closet years later.' I thought over what I had just said. He probably had a point. 'Uh! Okay. Maybe you are right.'

~

In my early thirties, during the India of the 1980s, these topics seemed utterly dry and boring. The sanctity of protecting cows and the heinousness of cow slaughter in a country that venerated them as mothers...the desire of the Hindu right-wing to implement its agenda of making religion the basis of nationhood and to build a near-theocratic state...building a mandir in Ayodhya...these were of little interest to most. Who on earth wanted lessons in history when one wanted to chat over a drink in the evening, listening to Elvis Presley or something romantic?

The cracks in our interests were beginning to surface before they ruptured and turned into schisms, slowly. Very, very slowly, till after many years, they became unbridgeable. We were apart in age by over a decade. He had seen the high life and was born into it. I wasn't. I was just beginning to be in the limelight and enjoying it. He was bored of it, knowing how fame, fortune and youth were ephemeral. I wanted to gossip about the party the night before, which irritated him. I wanted to dress up. He wanted to dress down. Life had a nobler and deeper purpose for him. I was like a hedonist, a hippie who wanted to savour the moment and live till the next party or next exotic holiday. He had seen the world. I had yet to explore it. I was a mall-rat who loved retail therapy, never wanting to repeat a saree. He was least interested in buying a new pair of shoes till they had a hole in them. I epitomized the nouveau Punjabi culture, while he epitomized 'old money'. I began to love partying till the wee hours of the morning, only to wake up by midday. He wanted to sleep early and wake before sunrise to do his yoga. He was from the world of old money, who felt no need to prove who he was through his material acquisitions. I had to be in-your-face, craving for the next acquisition of a new car or bauble.

I had a long way to go, though at the time I didn't think so. I had a lot of growing up and growing out to do.

Surya must have secretly felt he was saddled with a bimbo for the rest of his life, having to dumb down intellectually to connect to my wavelength. Poor him! But poor me too, because the novelty of wealth had not worn off and our frequencies were out of whack with each other.

~

The call to change

11 p.m.: 'I just received a call from the CM's office informing me Pita ji has been detained in UP and kept under house arrest. I have to gently break this news to the family. I am wondering whether to wake them up or let them know early morning tomorrow.'

'Oh my God! What for? What are you saying, Surya?' I trembled.

'Since his organization BHS was one of the proponents of resurrecting Ayodhya, his hate speeches against minorities were deemed inflammatory and cited as evidence of him being complicit in the conspiracy to bring down the mosque, along with many other members of the Parivar.'

'That's insane! How does it matter if we have a mandir/masjid/orphanage? Why did he have to crusade for such an inconsequential cause?' I asked.

'Stupid! Being a convent-educated nerd, this is beyond your grasp, Aksh. Forget it. All this will fly above your head. Go to sleep. I've had a talk with the authorities to ensure Pita ji's given VIP treatment in the guest house where he's under arrest so that they keep him comfortable.'

~

My reflections changed by the age of Modi

When I married Surya, there were raging debates within the family as Pita ji was considered the intellectual ancestor, one of the moral voices of the fifty-five associates of the Sangh, fanning passionate, populist sentiments through his demagoguery. Post-Partition, he had become a diehard member of the Hindutva brigade, always precluding his greetings with 'Bharat Mata ki Jai'. While other sects of the Sangh Parivar stood for the initial restoration of Ayodhya, Pita ji's BHS went beyond that symbolism of restitution of Hindu's rights, extending their activism to include reclaiming the holy shrine of Mathura–Kashi too. As a votary of building Kashi–Mathura–Ayodhya, he was amongst the many collective leaders who set out to undo the perceived historical injustices of Moghul invaders. Narendra Modi's landslide win in 2014 only emboldened the sense of Hindu renaissance and pride.

The Ram Janmabhoomi was only a symbol, a bold statement of intent by Hindu activists to reinstate their rights. If this was a deep sentiment of the Hindu majority, to rebuild what was believed to have been Bhagwan Ram's place of birth, ideally, minorities should have been gracious to concede and not resist this move. Could we Hindus ever claim in a Muslim country the same rights and privileges to practise our religion, considered, as we were, 'idol-worshippers', so openly? If anything, jizya, a tax on non-Muslims, was paid by the rest of the world who lived in Islamic states in the nineteenth century, other faiths being deemed infidels or kafirs. Non-Muslims are still excluded from occupying the highest authority in Islamic states, whether it's becoming a President or a Prime Minister, when Indians were secular enough to have gladly embraced three Muslim Presidents.

Pita ji felt religion and people's deep-rooted sentiments could not be adjudged by a court of law, and the solution lay outside even the apex court, which should have had no lien on it. Except that the ire of the masses, fed on an opium of religion to divert from governmental lapses, had spilled onto the streets, making it a matter of law and order. The sadhus felt the Ram temple was close to their hearts and would obstruct any move by the union government to act unilaterally. It was decided that the Akhara Parishad would, through bilateral talks, convince the Muslim religious leaders, and all four Shankaracharyas would participate in a bhumi puja to start the construction. Pure idealism! If only... As a trade-off, a masjid would be built with the help of Hindu religious leaders to appease the Sunni Waqf Board. That was the ideal solution, albeit as seen through the Hindu worldview.

In a widely heard radio interview, Pita ji echoed the sentiments of Hindu righteousness in building the Ram Janmabhoomi and said that the Godhra riots were intentional. If we were attacked, we had every right to counter-attack, echoing the sentiments of the majority community.

'Hindus are too tolerant. If we are attacked in our own country, we have every right to defend ourselves,' Pita ji said fearlessly in his interviews to the media.

While I observed all that was going on, I was beginning to feel proud of an illustrious lineage through marriage, one which I could not have remained isolated from or immune to. I felt like it was time to shed my secular stance and fake cosmopolitan persona. I also began to think like a kattar Hindu, as I felt we were too passive and far too submissive towards minorities. Why were we apologetic, pacifist and conciliatory in demeanour towards other religious sects in our home country? For fear of riots or selfish vote-bank appeasement by political parties? It was the minorities who had made an informed choice to be domiciled in a country that had a majority population of Hindus, wasn't it?

I had turned into an atheist through circumstantial defeat, refusing to partake of empty ritualism like visiting mandirs. But by the Age of Modi, the Hindu right-wingers had succeeded in drawing me back to my roots as a contagion of proud-to-be-Hindu was in the air, making me a neo-convert again. The 'ghar wapasi' of an atheist like me saw it as trendy to sound like an activist for cow slaughter and indulge in Muslim-bashing on Twitter. A new breed of puritanical Internet Hindus like myself was all over social media and God help you if you expressed secular sentiments in your comments! As Islamophobia gripped the world and the nation, the RSS, Sena or Modi-bhakts could maul you for straying out of line and troll you till you were dead. Death-by-Twitter? I never thought the power of a 140-character sting from someone I never knew, nor was ever likely to meet, could diminish me so severely for expressing even a neutral point of view, as it happened when I got trolled, 'U must be the illegitimate offspring of one of d Muslim invaders.' I sensed an orchestrated fear that was being instilled to inspire faith, as the tyranny of dogma was drowning the voice of reason, common sense or the spontaneous conviction of the individual. While a side of Modi was growing out of his RSS pracharak roots after his exposure to a global world, his tacit silence on the rabidity of the fringe elements within his party seemed an endorsement of archaism. Rationalists were being inked by bigots, spewing venom on them for their candour, while opposing the establishment could border on the seditious.

Champagne Dialogues and Shampoo Politics

2000 onwards

WHILST MY DIARIES are excerpts of intense ponderings on the years of my marriage to a scion of a prominent family of India, my reflections would be incomplete without an incisive look at the regalia within the highbrowed Lutyen's circle. Societal interactions have a deep impact on thoughts, impossible as it is to distance oneself from one's milieu. For the feeble-minded, if one does not have the tenacity to stand tall and firm in upholding one's authentic convictions, those liaisons can be an intimidating experience rather than supportive comfort. Most who have had close encounters with Delhi's haute monde will identify with my take.

I give it as it is…to paraphrase from the legendary Khushwant Singh, 'Without malice, fear or favour.'

~

I believe in the goodness of man and retain an implicit faith in knowing that human beings are born virtuous, innocent till proven guilty. Look into the spirit of most, and an effulgent light shines through, as we were made in the image of god to love and illuminate those whose world we impact.

But to my dismay and sadness, I sometimes put my faith in vultures. Vultures who prey on you when your morale is low, but feast with you in prosperous times. Some redundant relationships I should have pressed the 'delete' on, just faded from the earlier bonhomie of good times. In retrospect, I was relieved more than pained, as life took on a deeper meaning.

I had close encounters with people for whom networking was a religion. Initially it was hard to reconcile and though some losses saddened, they did not embitter me endlessly. I reasoned that not every seed bears fruition, and not every investment bears great returns. It was the same with friendships if two souls didn't necessarily evolve at the same pace.

In big cities it's a harsh and cruel man-eats-man world. 'Life in a Metro', in New York, London, Delhi... there exist well-defined hierarchies of power in societies. There is essentially a kingpin and a diva, and a descending order of their minions as the chain spirals downwards to the bottom of the barrel. I neither aspired to the kingpin altar nor wished to belong to this spiral in the top-down or bottom-up ladder, though I was endlessly bemused, voyeuristically watching the scene from the sidelines.

In a dynamic, ever-changing world, that wheel of fortune rotated swiftly in Delhi. The diva and kingpin status could reverse fast. 'Schadenfreude', a sadistic feeling of pleasure when misfortune strikes an opponent, was what the rest of the sycophants felt for the diva-and-kingpin duo when the flavour of the season changed in ranking order, synonymous with the Forbes billionaires list of the year.

In the primary stage of wealth creation, in one's first brush with affluence, an essential passport, the entry into The Hall of the (in-)Famous, was an obvious address in Lutyens' Delhi.

The essentials were ownership of a bungalow, a BMW car and a Hussain hanging on the wall, to list just a few. Of course, an affable, interesting persona, wit, power and glamour, were a given imperative to complete the social CV. If you lacked even one of the prerequisites, you never made the cut to the glitterati circus.

Oh yes! One more, and last but not the least in the ladder left to climb, was that one had to appear philanthropic and join a charitable organization. That made you an instant patron of the arts. If one held auctions for the underprivileged, it accelerated the climb to the top, gaining fast-track fame. An apt occasion to display virtuosity was at chauthas, funerals or marriages. There was no better occasion to show proximity to someone you aspired to become an appendage to in the social order. A designer wardrobe of lily whites and pastels, a white Chanel handbag and a perfectly rehearsed look for sombre condolences was the persona one donned for showing up at bereavements. Crumpled white clothes or dishevelled hair was shoddy dressing for commiseration.

I do offer a disclaimer. These were the known requisites for entering the Secret World and secret codes of conduct for conformity. If some nuance escaped me in this finishing school etiquette, I need to be forgiven my trespasses.

During the day, 9 a.m. to 7 p.m. when husbands toiled, was also peak office time for the kitty party circuit. You danced the afternoons away in the luring climes of Delhi winters, sipping Crystal champagne or green tea, whatever your nectar. Ladies' lunches were seldom at coffee shops for the highbrowed. Champagne and caviar lifestyles had upped that ambience to another level. Male strippers were the new objects of desire at these lunches, as the ageing auntie jis' voyeurism was insatiable, mine included! Band baajaa baaraat, from weddings to funerals, was a ritual of everyday life.

Bejewelled, bedecked, bemused and bored with 'The Bold and the Bountiful', for fifteen years I was pleasurably a part of this fraternity. The only point of being up-close and personal with the comely lot was that I came out feeling a mental bonsai. Silver service, gloved waiters, muted melodies and muted whispers with munificent hospitality was awesome but inadequate to sustain anyone who wanted to walk the road to a qualitative life. The penury of my own thoughts began to hit hard.

I wanted to walk away and walk alone. It might be a lonely journey but it was my chosen path. It was an informed choice. Surya sounded a wake-up call that made me sit up and smell the champagne! He asked me what my life's vision statement, my goals and my personal evolution was, five years from now? Ten years from now? Fifteen years from here? As we grow and evolve, there is a crying need to transcend the transitory. To cling to pleasures that appease the narcissism in one's self is a predatory desire, as one preys on sustenance from others. I never meant to sound derogatory or counter-elitist about this cult I engaged with. But I was determined not to live the rest of my life pursuing pleasures of the rich and famous, instead yearning to grow more whole, wholesome and rooted from within. I didn't care about the downside risk of being deemed a pariah. There was an inner world's treasure to discover, far deeper and more gratifying than this frivolous carnival, this play of 'maya', the cyclical play of illusions and delusions. I was not going to go to my grave foolish!

An obsessive love affair with one's self began with dispensing for the need for approval or dependency on a spouse, friends or society. Hobbies and work became essential for survival, as my self-worth did not stem from money and all that I could indulge in as a consequence of affluence.

I discovered a passion to express. Copious streams of thoughts I never paid attention to started pouring out of hidden crevices stored in my emotional memory. When I sat down to write, it was intoxicating when my pen raced faster than my flow. Pure moments of candour and confession. It became like a clandestine amour where I wanted to tell all, give it my all, freeing myself from my loves, hates, insecurities and fears. Free-spirited and unafraid, inebriated in that magical moment, I could not predict what my love affair with life would bring out…the good, the bad or the ugly.

Writing took time, as any creative pursuit or hobby requiring diligence and discipline. I created that time, abandoning sleep, people, television and family.

My altered perspective made adversaries dissolve, as neither people nor the goings-on in the external world penetrated that invincible fortress. Immersed in the ritual and discipline of creativity, baser emotions ebbed, faded and self-incinerated, as I became closeted in the sacredness of a passionate pursuit.

I found material needs diminished as cerebral inquiry and inquest took precedence. Despite being a creature of comfort, when I felt elated and complete in myself, I was not at my jewellers buying diamonds or in search of guilty pleasures that fanned my unrestrained narcissism.

I did all of that when I was half a woman, when I thought money could buy me love, friendships, immortality in lieu of transience. Older and more comfortable in my skin, it's a fleeting gratification, one I least covet. But this cycle of life would not have been complete had I not donned those acquired feathers for a while. They were acquired plumes that shed with the season.

I had to pass that route in my spiritual evolution in order to shed and relinquish it today. New plumage has grown, softer and purer in its stead.

I found nurturing my mind, body and soul more rewarding than pleasures that did not sustain or serve me anymore. I was no longer enslaved by the material, having trumped those futile urges. My restlessness quelled as did my competitive, rough edges. One competes for calibre or for intellectual prowess, but competing for status was a vacuous pastime.

I was grateful I had comforts beyond the normal. I thanked god in sincere humility for the privileged life I led. But just being wealthy was an inadequate credential for a claim to fame.

Part IV

The Black Swan Years

Twenty-two Years after Marriage

2009 onwards

Jab dhadkan ek dastak ki tarah goonjney lagee...

BLACK SWANS ARE ugly ducklings that lurk in corners and crevices when fortune favours man, rearing their ugly heads just when the going is good. Unexpected events occur in the life of man that derail, acting as saboteurs to all that is good and great, striking with such a ferocity that most are ill-prepared for the loss of love, the loss of a loved one or the loss of money.

My Black Swan years may not have struck with the suddenness that singular events afflict. But they were a gradual build-up of a lot that I held closest to my heart, which got swept in that relentless tide, eroding and snatching away what should have been the best years of my life, taking down with them all that I cherished.

Those were the blackest and darkest years I spent, imprisoned within its walls, without a ray of light, starting life all over again for the second time at middle age, staring at what befell upon me in utter helplessness. I was down on my knees in prayerful silence, with hands outstretched to The God of Small Things, to The God of Big Things...to The God of Anything... to mitigate the immensity of its force somewhere.

~

With the ascent of India on the global horizon, those years were also a time that witnessed the decline of the old business dynasties of independent Bharat. Not overnight, but very gradually. The mightiest were falling off the cliff. The myth of Icarus, who flew too close to the sun and crashed, came to mind. It was a change so swift it swept those virtual oligarchs off their monopolies, a price paid for being out of sync with a fast-paced, multipolar world that displaced the fiefs of yore nearly twenty years post liberalization.

In the early 1990s the Indian economy was in shambles and if the government did not liberalize, the International Monetary Fund would not provide the requisite funding for the economy to grow. The licence-quota-permit-raj was dismantled in favour of a free market economy with cosy cartels of Indian businesses facing competition from global competitors. The process of dismantling Indira Gandhi's socialist controls that strangled growth had begun, throwing Indian industrialists who thus far lived under protectionism to the vagaries of global trade.

Not coping well with globalization, what worsened the recovery was the economic downturn of 2008.

Consequently, with Surya preoccupied with devoting more time to business and staying away for longer periods from home, I felt we were drifting further apart, because he communicated lesser and lesser as time went by. I had little to do sitting at home by myself, while he turned quieter, aloof and snappy during the little time we spent together. He never cared to address my growing misconceptions, from feelings of isolation to suspicions of betrayal, as we hardly dialogued. In hindsight, I was oblivious to his pressures stemming from business concerns, as much as he was insensitive to my aloneness, which eventually drove us both to a simmering point.

I yearned to step off the ramp of the glitzy world in quest of simplicity, which made me leave my Hermes and Jimmy Choos undusted on their racks, much as one symbolically leaves one's shoes outside a sacred shrine before entering its holy precincts. Shed, shed, shed. Shed my ego, shed my vanity, shed my yearning to hold on to a marriage that was no marriage.

Life's play had chipped away at my ego, peeling at it layer by layer, transforming me into a 'millionaire nun' in search of an alternate state of being. I questioned myself time and again, year after year, if I was content to remain a footnote to a celebrity husband, subsumed by his grandeur, reduced to being just an invisible partner. I yearned to revert to a period of productivity when I worked my way up the professional ladder as a working woman, during my HCL days, two decades back.

↝

Living between two houses, sometimes a night here and sometimes at the Mittal House, when I would get to see less of Surya, I once said, 'Dear, are you out for dinner tonight also? Must you go?' I was to learn as time went by that women in feudal households don't ask for more than what is revealed to them.

'Why? Why do you quiz me almost daily!' he exclaimed.

'Oh sorry, because I wanted to make a meal for you that you would love...'

'Akshraa, please don't snoop. If I am home you will see me, I am not invisible.'

'But, honey, I hardly get to see you in the evenings for days on end. You are turning scarce and I barely see you in this house. You just breeze in and out and I am left sitting by myself not only in the day when you are at work but most evenings too, of late. It gets a little lonely, you know. If you are so busy in the evenings, can I at least utilize my past professional competence at work and join you in business? I promise you won't regret giving me responsibilities in any one of the many companies you own. I will do you proud and add value. It might take me time to get inducted but I will learn the ropes. Could you consider that, please?' I had requested for this intermittently from time to time over many years, feeling that I was imploring a master as an unequal, only to be rejected again.

'Silly idea,' he snubbed me.

'No, no! Please don't turn me down. Please just see what a beautiful multi-storied venture I did with Mr Bansal, a leading architect. My parents' property in West End, which you have seen as a ramshackle bungalow on 1,000 square yards, was razed to the ground and turned into a state-of-the-art residence that yields me a fortune. Surya, you own prime land on the outskirts of Delhi, Mumbai and Bangalore. It's all lying undeveloped. Please hand it over to me as a project. I promise to make it a money spinner,' I carried on enthusiastically, camouflaging my feelings of hurt at the rejection yet again. 'At least I will get to see you at office in the day, if not in the evenings,' I implored, thinking I had arrived at a great formula to bridge the gaps.

'Akshraa, my family will oppose it. I don't need a business feud with them now! My answer is no. Traditional Indian families don't welcome women being active participants in business. No other woman has worked in our family, so neither will you. That's final.'

Some weeks later I was surprised to see that he had a change of heart and asked me to build a nice study-cum-working room at home. He even gave me a staff of two to assist me. I realized that it was more to give me a place to operate out of instead of allocating me space at his corporate headquarters that would avert any possible collision with his brother Arvind.

Real estate was not one of the Mittals' core businesses. Acres of land which surrounded his factories lay idle and undeveloped. So he didn't mind giving me responsibility in what he thought would be an untapped, unexplored venture, more like a way for me to pass time and get me off his back.

Coincidentally, a boom had begun in real estate almost all across India. I wanted to prove my worth and make a mark after years of idle socializing and being a bored stay-at-home wife. He sent across the title papers, the maps and layouts of the land in Bangalore, his smallest property in size and value, as I immersed myself, happy to learn the ropes of a new vertical. My depression at home because of being alone most of the day was bringing me down. I motivated myself and after meeting several builders, zeroed in on Mr Rajagopal Reddy, the largest in Bangalore, to develop Surya's tiniest land parcel, which was a locked godown that had been inoperative for many years. It was under 3 acres and valued at around ₹30 crore if sold outright. Reddy had a good track record of financials and was known to deliver projects on schedule, providing the best quality in malls and commercial establishments.

After negotiations and before signing the deal, I took it to Surya for his approval. Mr Reddy had developed a business plan for how many square feet could come out of this plot and had worked on the yields if we part-sold and part-retained the balance for rentals. It could accrue handsome profits and could become a project valued at over ₹160 crore over two years if the real-estate boom continued. Or even at worst, if it remained stable, the value could fall marginally below this figure.

Gleeful, I knew Surya would applaud my endeavours and

the potential I had identified. I knew this way I could show him that his trust in me was well placed. I was excited and arranged a meeting between the builder and him to close this deal. He sat in on the meeting and took great interest in Mr Reddy's presentation. After it concluded, he shook hands and said, 'I will get back to you in a few weeks. It sounds good but I want to think a little more. Akshraa may not be directly involved but I will instruct my project heads to liaise with you if we do take a decision to conclude the deal. It was a pleasure meeting you.'

I saw Mr Reddy to the door and told Surya I would meet him at home at his usual hour around 7 p.m.

I couldn't wait for Surya to come and applaud me on striking gold on a closed godown. He stormed into our room in a temper as I was sipping tea on my bed, staring vacantly at the garden my bedroom overlooked, least expecting I could have been the cause of his wrath. 'Akshraa, I don't trust you. A member of my family has told me that you've struck a deal with this builder on the side to siphon out a few crores. You thought I would never get to know, right? Anyway, please return all the files and documents to me tomorrow. You want to pilfer from your own husband's company!'

'Surya, no. No, no, no. If anything, I only want to be an asset to you...'

'I want my papers back, do you hear me? My family had cautioned me about marrying a girl from a middle-class family and how greed would get the better of her when she sees affluence she isn't otherwise exposed to.' I ran to my small office and collected all the files to give them to him immediately. He didn't take them. Instead, he rudely snatched what I was holding in my hands. With that, he snatched not only the documents but the little self-respect and confidence I had left. It was demeaning.

It was the most painful night I spent with myself, being called a thief and an embezzler of his company funds. I was defenceless against his suspicions, pronounced guilty in my own home.

His brother Arvind and the family had ganged up yet again to put me down and ensure I had no say in the joint family business. I had to heal myself, take a deep breath and just let go.

The assault occurred with brutal words that stabbed my heart. There were no illusions left from here on. It's the way a child's universe of fantasies crumbles when the reality of Santa Claus and tooth fairies being myths strikes! There was nothing more to see, nothing more to know. This was a dead end, a closed door to a chapter of my life.

This was my personal and emotional 26/11! Three days after the anniversary of the fatal terror attacks in Mumbai, a day etched in memory, ripples reverberated in a demolition of my own little world. Life was never the same for us hereafter.

I reached an emotional watershed that day, as my doll's house broke forever.

A tale of two decades ended with an abruptness that haunts me even now. I walked on glass from there on, with rubble under my feet on an avalanche of ruins for many, many years before capitulating and making sense of what befell upon me at midlife.

~

Diana, Princess of Wales, once said about her embittered marriage with Prince Charles and his covert affections, 'There were three of us in this marriage, so it was a bit crowded...' We all know her tribulations of getting accepted into a royal household as a commoner. She became the patron saint of women married into aristocracy, who broke from the duplicity and agony of palace intrigues, ecstasy be damned! It was about one's own pride over prejudice, the prejudice of the blue-blooded over plebs. I aligned and hugely emoted with those scarred feelings.

Coming as I did from an upper middle-class family, the basic codes were non-negotiable. The high life didn't charm or anchor me enough. I use the phrase 'middle class' because it is a matter of bourgeois pride that they took pleasure in simple living and high thinking that money could not buy.

There is enshrined in the heart of every woman an unspoken need for love, caring and dignity, a deeply monogamous instinct to have her man belong to her.

I wondered how the rich dealt with grief in public or private, as memories of another day, of the last century raced past my mind, of a Hillary Clinton who went past public humiliation and betrayal by a husband who was the most powerful man on earth. She turned to being on perpetual political overdrive, perhaps using ambition as a drug to numb her pain. Perhaps it was heartening to know that the rich and powerful possessed base emotions much the same as commoners, whether a poor woman cried in a hut or a princess in her palace; whether the rich drowned their woes over single malts or the poor did so with country liquor.

My coping mechanism was to turn insular and inwards. I was like a junkie in search of her next fix. I lived on chicory and nicotine; got my adrenaline from gymming and the stock markets; my serotonin from learning Bollywood dancing and meditation. I don't think any of them really healed but they did repress a wailing heart, as I began to levitate with those momentary escapes.

A Farewell to Love: Adieu, My Beloved, till We Meet Again

IT NEVER RAINS but it pours, as the saying goes. While Surya and I were growing irreconcilably apart, I was shuttling between Mumbai's Saifi hospital, where Mummy had slipped into a coma, and Delhi. I oscillated between two sad worlds making it the most trying period of my life. Strain at home, knowing twenty years of marriage were at a near-end, and weekly visits to Mumbai to see my mother who was fading.

Room 501 in the ICU had become my temporary abode in the luxurious hospital run by an affluent sect of Bohri Muslims. Piped music, murals, fountains, a hospital with aesthetic overtones, came as a comforting, even though momentary, sensual relief to the pain that lay ahead. Mummy's room overlooked the ocean waves, as the haunting lyrics, '*Tu dhaar hai nadiyaa ki, main tera kinaraa hoon; Jeewan ka matlab toh aana aur jaana hai*', replayed through my mind.

My mother on life support whilst my life with Surya was on the ventilator.

Each time I left the room I would turn back to see my mother's peaceful face before shutting the door, just in case it was the last time. For those three months, every call on my mobile was like a call from Hades. I dreaded the shrill ring. For whom the bell tolls…for whom the gods love, young or old, and whose turn it is for them to summon, mortals never do know.

Till the inevitable happened after I had just landed in Delhi. As I switched on my mobile in the aircraft, there were six missed calls, then a text. 'Dr Chichkar here, Akshraa. I have to break it to you. Mom won't live to see tomorrow. It's any time now. So brace yourself and start with the rituals, organize a family priest. Its 4 p.m., so it gives you enough time. See me in her room asap.'

'Doctor, I've just returned from Mumbai… I will take the next flight back.'

Physically and emotionally drained, my heart thumped and my knees went weak as I boarded the flight back to Mumbai and headed for the hospital. 'Akshraa, you are a brave girl. I've come to pay my last respects to your mother. Trust me, my team and I did the best to revive her. God be with you. Do keep in touch,' the doctor said. I walked into Mummy's room for the last time and kissed her on her ice-cold forehead before other relatives poured in. My last chance at a private farewell. They say a few hours after a soul departs it can see and hear the weeping and wailing of anguished ones surrounding the body. I chose to believe that and said to her softly, 'Thank you, Mama. You are our Queen Mother. Thank you for all your sacrifices, ones we can never repay in lifetimes to come. Silent night, holy night, sleep in heavenly peace. Mama, I love you and God can never make another you. I will abide by every instruction you gave me to the last bugle call. I love you, Mama. Farewell, for this lifetime, till we meet again.'

The next morning the last rites were performed whilst Surya cradled me in his arms and held my hand firmly through the ceremony. As final as Mummy's departure was, I knew Surya's embrace too had a finality, that his hand was trying to subtly extricate from mine, ease its way out of my cold palms.

I proceeded to Haridwar the following day, resting the terracotta urn that held my mother's ashes on my lap in the flight, clinging on to her mortal remains for life before going on to perform the last rites. Steeped in sorrow, I felt exposed to a parentless world, unprotected by a spouse who had hinted at an impending separation.

It was exactly eight years ago that I had stood at the same spot to bid adieu to my father's mortal remains. I reminisced how with deepest sorrow I had poured the ashes with my hands gently into a small vessel, sprinkled some marigold flowers, lit a diya and lay them on the lap of the sacred Ganga. The river's torrential speed drove the vessel with swift fury...Daddy on his onward journey...gone. Swept away by the river's unrelenting tide with the finale of the lingering chants of the sacred Gayatri mantra recited by the pundits: '*Om bhoor bhuva swaha*.'

Copious tears flowed down my cheeks as Surya held me close to his chest and said, 'Aksh, I know how bereft you are, being Dad's favourite child. I can never replace him but I solemnly vow that I will continue to give you the unconditional love he gave you so you know you are never, ever alone. I am whisking you away for three days to an exotic palace, an hour away from London, the Cleveland Palace. I have booked the presidential suite for us. It's a sprawling 7,000 square feet expanse which you will love. We will be together, one with nature amidst a luxurious escape. I won't take no for an answer. You need to get away. We are heading back to Delhi and you will finish your packing as we are booked on BA for 1 tonight. Now give me a smile?' Those were sentiments expressed in happier days when he felt my pain.

Today, with my second parent gone, I realized Surya's sympathy was a charade. It was a lie. He had had a change of heart over the years to abide by his commitment. Nothing was forever. Eight years later, I wondered what happened to those solemn promises. Transient emotions, said out of pity?

But pity was never reason enough to stay on in a loveless marriage. Compassion? Duty? Nothing was enough to hold on this time around. I had no time to grieve this huge loss. He was uncaring enough to abandon me and my brood three months later. Swift and abrupt, it pierced my heart, like the stabbing cut of a surgical knife. After the last rites were performed, my son and I drove up to the Glass House on the Ganges in Rishikesh, just an hour uphill, owned by a very dear friend. So utterly soothing in the most dismal times, she was like a tranquillizer who had the effect of calming the most frayed nerves.

Meera said, 'Trust me, this too shall pass, Aksh. Mourn mom's passage, grieve deeply for that loss which is a void no one can ever replace. Weep. Wail. But don't grieve after Surya. He is unworthy of you. Deal with the demise of a mother. But the death of love? A man who heartlessly wants to walk out on you… bury those memories forever, they don't warrant your tears. I promise you, sweetie, a day will come when you will look back at your achievements with pride. Cherish them… In comparison to how tall you stand, Surya is a speck! Now, can I give you a small glass of wine? Let's celebrate the full life Auntie lived, shall we? And talk of her momentous life? She was a grand lady!'

Meera had reserved two of the quaintest cottages adjoining each other, one for me and one for Vishal. Both of them were located right on the Ganges, a few yards away from where one could hear the torrid gush of the river's flow and view it streaming past the cottage. Utterly serene.

I tossed and turned. The first night ever in my life without my mother. How would life be from here on without her? After her? What would she say to me if she was around and knew of Surya abandoning me? How would she have mentored me? Knowing her sense of dignity, she would never have let me succumb.

My parents believed they left me in good hands and saw me well settled. I am, in a way, thankful that those were the abiding memories that must have stayed in their hearts before they left for their journey home. I had orchestrated it such that they never knew the downside to my relationship with Surya.

To bear the burden of a child's grief is living death for any parent. Being a great actress I feigned happiness, veiling my deepest sorrows so as not to burden them in their twilight years. Besides, there is little they could have done to mitigate my sorrows if those were the karmic debts I was born with and was ordained to pay back in this lifetime.

~

Strangely, treasures of Mama's sagely wisdom came like disguised messages.

'Akshri-yaa, I am no more with you in body, beta. But I will hold your hand and see you through this impending doom. Please never feel forsaken, my gudiyaa. You are not to feel disempowered if Surya walks out on you. Live tall, walk tall, the way we raised you! You are educated and well-fortified with assets Daddy and I have left you to never have to bow your head before insolent might. For the fortune we have left you with, may you multiply it 1,000 times over with your own financial wisdom to never have to stretch your hands to anyone. I want you to never, ever surrender on demeaning and unequal terms even in a marriage.'

I had to heal myself, take a deep breath and just let go. I

knew the end of this marriage was near because staying on had little honour left. I had to quit someday.

~

The following morning, I was surprised to hear from Zaheer Khanna, the banker acquaintance I had met in Davos. He had read the obituary and wanted to call on me. I was touched by his text but told him I was in Rishikesh for a few days. I didn't make much of it…other than it being a small courtesy. It did bring a smile to my face though. A tiny reprieve after a tearful night.

I eagerly awaited the birth of my first grandchild two months later. Steeped in sadness, numbed with pain, I must admit I was guilty of not being wholly present in the now of his momentous arrival. It was all a haze, so blinded was I at that time to be aware of the biggest gift God was giving me.

In rapid succession, the loss of a parent, the loss of a lifetime gone by with Surya. Then the arrival of an angelic being fortunately ignorant of the family circumstances he was born into.

'Turning and turning the world goes round, you can't change it, my friend.'

Sometimes circumstances and events occur in such rapid succession, at such a furious pace, the senses can't absorb them as there is no pause to feel the intensity of those accompanying sensations of joy or sorrow.

A Fight for Survival

I HAD LIVED through most travails of my life with reasonable equanimity. At least I had tried to do so putting my stoic best foot forward. After going through the cyclical gamut of hope and despair, there followed a period of levelling out. I wasn't going to stoop for a paltry stipend called alimony, as the dispensation of justice in India was a prolonged and treacherous wait.

Immodestly, if I may say so, I was quite a princess at heart. I thought it below my class to slum it, to wear an old cotton saree and play to the gallery of judges the role of an impoverished wife in an attempt to evoke their sympathy. Drama queen I was but not interested enough to play tragedy queen for sure. 'How utterly déclassé,' I told myself. If I should have been given what was rightfully a wife's due, it should have been served on a silver platter and not be seen squatting on a wooden bench at the courts awaiting a judge to determine my allowance! So uncool, I felt!

What a waste of time to frequent non-air-conditioned courts in the sultry heat of Delhi and trek through paint-chipped, cobwebbed corridors, stinking with the odour of smelly loos, just to fight for a financial settlement! Surely, there were easier, more intelligent ways to compensate making a livelihood.

I was educated and well-informed, though my knowledge and skills needed updating, rusted as they had become with being a subservient housewife for so many years.

My self-image mattered more to me than societal strictures or norms. Surya was well aware of the aristocratic propensity I was predisposed to, knowing I would not put in an effort at chasing a stipend. It was too infra dig to be fighting any man for livelihood and shelter. I honestly had better things to do than to look backwards.

Alimony to me was like looking for a poor consolation prize in lieu of love. When either spouse loves with purity, to be compensated with money and assets, though a rightful plea by a wife, was a paltry substitute for a lifetime gone by when cash could never be a substitute for love, respect and honour two people shared in wedlock.

~

Reflections thereafter

In the patriarchal society we live in, men mostly control the family's financial resources. More than three-quarters of Indian women do not even hold a bank account. Per capita access to bank credit is also far lower for women than men.

When I look back in hindsight at those years of strife, I would implore any woman, regardless of her marital status or economic strata, to learn that the key to surviving any vicissitudes in life lay in understanding the science of money: financial literacy. Aside from endorsing a sense of purpose to life, knowing the art of savings from trickles of earning and then compounding that to constitute wealth would make any woman stand tall.

I often lived in fear—would I remain a puppet to the whims and fancies of the breadwinner, the karta of the family? I was reasonably educated but not skilled in any particular sphere.

My career paths opened up by sheer luck in my earlier years when I was in my twenties, as I became an accidental professional out of utter boredom, more to get away from ladies luncheons, kitty parties and the vacuous life of the rich and famous who idled the rest of their time shopping or playing cards at a neighbouring club once their children were of school-going age.

As life unfolded, my security stemmed wholly from the savings I had made in a very disciplined way. It empowered me to be unbending and secure in the might of never compromising to what felt against my grain even in a marriage. I saved and created wealth by building a sound corpus. I invested in a property which was the roof over my head and a separate one that was a source of monthly income. Cumulative wealth grew to yield further compounding gains as the money tree bore fruit.

❧

It took me a long, long while to reconcile as I moved from anguish to denial, to resignation, through an endless dark tunnel. The force majeure events that crumbled my little world left me immobilized with only two choices: to either bury my head like an ostrich or rise like a phoenix and recreate my world, piece by piece.

Fear and greed, jealousy and anger are the primordial, primitive instincts of womankind. They are the base instincts of survival. They can annihilate if one dwells in that space for too long, or hugely empower if one conquers them. I would be lying if I did not admit to oscillating furiously in that territory. Gradually, I watched myself grow, not harden.

Servility and passivity gave way to courage to embrace change and take it on the chin, 'Where the mind is without fear and the head is held high…' I refused myself the luxury of wallowing in grief or going down a dark alley of recrimination.

Those were the cards dealt to me. Some hands I played badly and some with great finesse, learning from my blunders.

I embarked on a huge image and personality makeover in middle age, post my split, upping my emotional, spiritual and financial quotient like a true student of life. I counted my blessings of my son and daughter-in-law, truly avatars of Sita and Ram, and my two little Krishnas, Viraj and Armaan.

As a caregiver to these rising stars I solemnly pledged to pursue a life of higher thought forms, a life beyond me. There comes a point when we begin to derive joy from living through the next generation. If god had willed me to be a mother and father, a grandmother and grandfather, just how privileged was I?

It was imperative to enlarge my universe beyond my personal tribulations. With the demise of a patriarch of the family the onus of setting traditions falls on the next incumbent. Life had to go on, so love and laughter, mirth and music had to be brought back into our home to feel the ripples of normalcy.

The Summer of '42: The Audacity to Love at any Age?

2013

IT WAS A hot summer morning around 7 a.m. in May. I hadn't frequented my second home, the gym at Amatra, which was located within The Ashok, in three weeks. Bored of the monotony of working out indoors, I decided to head to Lodi Gardens which was just across my home. One needed to alternate as workouts get dull and boring if they are the same each day. People tend to exercise closest to where they live, so both the venues were conveniently equidistant for me.

At Lodi, one invariably came across a mix of bureaucrats, ministers, industrialists, oldies and youngsters, all of whom were busy meditating or doing yoga, or a group of veterans who had joined a laughing club, or brisk walkers, eager to kick-start their day before heading to work. No one had time to stop and exchange courtesies as it slowed down the pace of walking. Even if one came across one's closest friend, a smile or hello was accepted protocol, an adequately cordial mannerism to brush past each other on the walking track.

The morning walkers at Lodi Gardens comprised a happy lot of veterans, those jolly-good-fellow uncles who would later go back home to enjoy a hearty desi Punjabi breakfast of aloo paranthas after a chatty walk with their comrades.

I was tickled pink coming across our now illustrious finance minister Arun Jaitley, surrounded by fifteen friends who comprised his entourage in tow, though he wasn't the Finance Minister then. In the now of 2015, being in eminence, the difference was that I recently saw him circled by a huge outer ring of heavy security. An eager beaver with headphones, greatly preoccupied, walked past at a pace that nearly threw me clumsily off my track. I was about to turn around and give him an angry glare. It was Zaheer Khanna and it had been a few years since we last met, with no contact in between other than a text condoling mom's passing away. My irritation mellowed to a smile. 'Akshraa! What are you doing here? I've been a regular in Lodhi for a decade but I have never seen you around here.'

'One of those freak instances. I was tiring of Amatra, my health club, so I pushed myself for a walk in the fresh air instead of walking on a treadmill in air-conditioned comfort.'

I was a slower walker than Zaheer. He was polite enough to measure his pace to match mine so we could take a round or two together, stamina levels permitting. 'I go to the gym at Aman Hotel in the evenings after work, around eightish. Mornings are always at Lodi Gardens. Why don't you switch to my gym?' he asked.

'Because Rahul Gandhi and Robert Vadra work out there? Uff! Baba, it's too highfalutin. Sorry, I'm just kidding. Zaheer, I am addicted to the ambience of Amatra. The trainers are really good and so is the equipment. Why don't you change your membership instead? It's a very fun-loving crowd,' I suggested.

'Chalo, let me give it a thought. How is Mr Mittal? I would love to meet him someday if you think it's okay. Maybe he could consider banking with us too.'

'Zaheer, we split a while ago.'

He seemed taken aback and confused about how to react. We had finished two rounds and I had reached the point where my car was parked.

'I wouldn't have thought or even guessed that! I had a glimpse of both of you, so together in Davos! I'm sorry to hear about the split. Anyway… it was great seeing you. Let's meet up one of these days? I will give you a call sometime this week, if I may? See you soon, I hope.'

❧

In my teens, I had seen the film *The Summer of '42*. Was that what was now playing out in my life? That story revisited?

Quite simply, I had a hazy recall of the plot being about an older woman in a twist with a man half her age. Torrid. Raunchy. How could there have been chemistry with such a bizarre and inverted age difference? Do these things happen in real life? What brings on such absurd attractions? Was it fiction, fantasy, chemistry-gone-wrong or sheer perversity? Or an ageing woman's desire to re-endorse her femininity? That she was good at any age to love again?

I was fifty-two years of age, vintage in a way like old wine matures, full-bodied and mellow. But my heart still beat to a youthful drum. I wondered, does love or the craving for it ever wane and ebb with age or does it amplify and get more pronounced, more haunting, more compelling than in a woman's youth?

A Jackie Kennedy syndrome? The middle-aged widow was quite a diva and style icon in her era, unrelenting in her quest for fame, power and marriage even after her president-husband's assassination. One who didn't mind giving up the most famous surname in the world, 'Kennedy', to take on the Greek tycoon Onassis's family name. Anything for love, I thought. Neither was a sin, nor a crime, if that's where her heart took her. For that matter, a Princess Diana would have gladly relinquished her royal married name for an Arab Dodi Fayed had they lived on, a notch below royalty, no doubt, in consenting to wed the richest commoner! A woman's primal need is to be loved, so all was fair in giving it a second chance, I reflected.

It's a crescendo when one is at crossroads. Inflection points and introspective milestones call for tough decisions. To pause and look back at my voyage this far, still craving a primordial urge for a relationship, my initial reactions were a bit self-flagellating. I was embarrassed to face up to a kind of compulsive desire to even feel attraction just two years since my bereavement at the death of my marriage.

I must admit, though, that in the last two decades the rules of love had changed! And if one was seeking a relationship, the mindset would have to be tweaked to the contemporary ways of thought. Society had turned less judgmental in gossiping, thinking little about casual sex or live-ins. Commitments were valid only for the now, and there was nothing contractual about these transitory attractions.

Zaheer called frequently thereafter, warming up to me with moves I found winningly irresistible.

'Akshraa, would it be too much if we exchanged pins for BlackBerry messenger? I care to know a bit more about you... That's if you don't misunderstand this overture?'

A younger man's modus and moves were so different from candlelight dinner dates and old-fashioned, slow and measured ways men went about a date in the 1980s. By 2013, it was a no-time-to-waste, crisp and calibrated manner of striking a rendezvous. Very to the point.

'Umm, sure, Z. It's P 215x66. I would love to be friends. You must know I am on a rebound and hurting… Whatever remains of me, I will emote. But there are boundaries we will draw from day one! As I am older, I will not enter a field where I might wreck you. That onus is on my shoulders… Anyway, I love the freshness of your energy. It is stimulating…'

We encountered each other at parties sitting across a packed room. He would text me sweet nothings! Love in 2013…exciting and ever so exhilarating, after the last ten years of my marriage had been so stressful. 'Aksh, how do you feel about a one-on-one dinner at the Waterfront at Aman Hotel? I know we've never met alone except at houses of common friends. May I take the liberty, if you are up for it tonight, say around 9ish?' he asked me one day.

I was flattered and flummoxed. Should I even be entertaining the thought of going out so brazenly, that too the first time he asked? 'Zaheer, let's make it a sundowner. Say 7ish instead of dinner, if we may? I am good with a drink and happy to skip dinner.'

'Done deal, Aksh. Catch you at 7!'

I got into a tizzy about what to wear on my first date with a young lad. Power dressing and donning serious jewellery I wore to diva dinners was passé. It would look too severe and a little intimidating, if not opulent and old, to be dressed in OTT (over-the-top) finery. I decided to opt for a girlish, young look in candy colours with trendy gypsy earrings and an oversized sporty watch, and I was done. I wanted to set a casual, fun, warm and playful tempo to an evening I began to count down towards. A bit nervous, even at the ripe age of fifty-two, I was as shy as I was on my first teenage date. I must have looked at my watch and mirror every few minutes, willing time to fly. It felt like an obsessive compulsive disorder afflicting me. This was a new experience, decking and dolling up for an amorous evening after an ennuied marriage. I had such low self-esteem I never cared to spruce myself up for Surya, who was usually too tired, preoccupied or disinterested to notice me.

Zaheer had style on his fingertips. Amidst this ritzy-glitzy restaurant, he'd reserved the most exclusive private room that protruded on to a waterbody. And from within that water, fire mashaals lit up the night sky. Utterly conducive for a tête-à-tête. Welcoming me with a warm embrace, he gave me a peck on the cheek, 'Aksh, this fragrance is divine. What are you wearing? It sits so well on you.'

'Thank you. It's Eau du Soir by Sisley. I drench myself in it. It's a real winter cologne, that too a winter evening one. My signature aroma. If you ever get a whiff of it even a few yards away, you'd know I am spooking or hovering around. Ha ha!'

'What's your poison?' he asked.

'May I please have a simple Black Label on the rocks? I don't want to sound uppity, but I am not into super premiums like Blue Label or single malts.'

'It's the same with me. I enjoy BL too. I must tell you, I am more of a social drinker. During weekends, though, I don't count my drinks. Then again, I am disciplined through the week. I avoid partying hard on weekdays as I prefer waking up early to get to Lodhi Gardens in time for my walk.'

'You know, Zaheer, I find people who over-socialize and drink too much are seriously flawed humans who don't know how to spend time with themselves. I love my routine too, though I don't hesitate to indulge in occasional deviations. Unless I must.

Like today...I felt like hanging out with you, so big deal!'

'Akshraa, may I put you at ease? I have no agenda for this evening except to warm up to you and get to know you a bit more. Let me tell you at the outset, I have been out with a lot of women closer to my age group. I was married to one for two years. Thereafter, some were serious encounters...but I guess I've shied away from most, as I was commitment-phobic. I am a fairly focused, serious guy. I'm a workaholic to a fault, highly ambitious to get to the top. Self-made, self-driven and self-funded with no leverage. What I do possess is an abundance of intellectual capital even if I say so without sounding modest. I dabble in commodities and property in a reasonable way in my personal assets, though I head Credit Suisse, as I told you in Davos. I could go on, but in a capsule, that's me, for preliminaries.'

'Z, that's a highly volatile space you are in! You are probably glued to your screen 24X7?'

'Yup. You've got to be alert round the clock because when India sleeps, the Nasdaq in New York's chiming. And when America's shutting down, Japan and China are about to rise and shine.'

'Got it! I'm impressed. I dabbled in 2011 in bullion too, or should I say, I foolishly punted. I saw the rise and rise of gold and silver as the dollar weakened. But I was lucky I quit the commodities market while the party was still on and before the crash and carnage that ensued.'

'Clever woman. So you do have some knowledge of the world of finance. Would you care to share with me at all which point of your personal life you are at, if I don't sound too intrusive?' he inquired.

'Asked with the sincere concern I see in your eyes, Zaheer, I don't mind giving you a candid answer. I am an open book.

I don't play mind games, power games, or damsel-in-distress games to stir sympathy. I was shattered after my marriage of twenty-three years ended. I am a monogamous kind of girl. I didn't have the wherewithal to suffer serial hurt and that was the beginning of the end for me...'

'Does that mean you would shut your eyes to any form of a relationship today?'

'Not necessarily, Zaheer. Unlike you, I am not commitment-phobic. I would give myself like a rabbit to anyone who stroked me with tender loving care. I don't over-analyze too much. I believe what you see is what the other person is. You could think that's naïve, I think it's trusting! Maybe that's why I am sitting opposite you, playing footsie with a virtual stranger in the night, a la Frank Sinatra.' I guess the little girl in me still clamoured for romance and felt alive doing so. In the depths of my heart, whatever the outcome with Zaheer, I felt a girlish enthusiasm that was beginning to eclipse the suffering and defeat of years gone by in semi-isolation. His spark was reigniting a euphoria.

'Akshraa, that I am drawn to you hugely I can't camouflage. Your persona is fire... Scorching, animated and witty, you come across as someone who is not bitter or cynical, a woman who wants to give love another chance. As to where this is leading, did one ever open a novel and know what was the ending? The epilogue? Can we treat this as a prelude to something beautiful to unfold? Say, a little less than an affair, a little more than a cosy crush?'

'It warms my heart, Z. You've made me an offer I am compelled to ponder on. Let's not have preconditions and give each other oodles of space. And let us know this enamour has a shelf life. Yes, I am on the rebound but that's not meant to burden your young shoulders. Those are my personal crosses to carry. As much as I know, grief doesn't last a lifetime, nor do attractions, though both are near-fatal experiences. The dilemma is to figure out where to put the commas and the full stops. It is a finite relationship defined by boundaries we don't cross, as there is no future to all this deep emotion. Wasted, in a way! I am sure you are aware.'

Back home by 11 p.m. I changed and curled under my duvet, slipping into a dreamy state, when I heard my BlackBerry ping. The red light on it was flashing. It was a message from him, 'Aku, I didn't want the evening to end. I wished it went on, stretched a little longer, so I could have had a wee bit more of you. You leave me breathless with your poise… your inner beauty captivates even more… I only promise you one thing, I will only come as close to you as you allow me, never violating you in mind, body or soul. Do you trust me on that?' The text had a solemn message; I couldn't help replying, 'Hmm! It might come as a surprise but I have been ruminating quite a bit over you…The boundaries I talked of are those the mind draws. My heart has none…Take care and catch you sooner rather than later, Z. Thanks for a great evening.'

Gentle and soft-spoken, with perfectly measured cadences in his tone, Zaheer gripped me with his compassion more than his looks. The spaces between his silence and intense glances spoke a lot. After his failed marriage, he was probably pitching for a new love that could fill his void. He was a refreshing contrast to the Punjabi-pappu-mama's-boys who lived off the wealth of their lineage but made little of their own. These were the brash youngsters who roamed around in limos followed by hired security cavalcades only to show off their petty importance; power-shooters who epitomized money, power, drugs and the venality of a debauched kind. Every facet of their persona, or lack thereof, was curated to smack of labels and brands that screamed wealth.

In a seductive tease, we played mental footsie on and off, sometimes through gestures and very often with words, that kept the attraction animated. 'You, Akshraa, are any man's sensuous dream,' he cooed. 'Akshraa, every time I hold your hand, you yank it away. What's your problem!'

❧

'Hi, Aku. It has been a black Monday. The dollar scaled sixty-four to the rupee! There's been a bloodbath across every asset class from equity to debt to commodities. Worse, the policymakers haven't a clue how to fix it. These cyclical turmoils are playing havoc with investors. I thought I would buzz you for an upper, a cigarette break and chat with you?'

'OMG! Yes, I've been glued to the screen too watching the mayhem. First these Americans wreck their own economy and the world's. Then they print more money and flush liquidity into the system at dirt cheap interest rates, causing a bubble. Now, they want to withdraw the stimulus. The contagion is being felt worldwide for the second or third time now! Zaheer, as good times don't last, I am sure the dust will settle after this too. But I do understand it's a precarious situation. Now to change the topic, I'll tell you what, I was always taught by nuns that "girls never make the move and ask boys out". May I break that norm and ask you if we can meet for another sundowner at the same time, but at Threesixty Degrees at The Oberoi?'

'Sounds good. I am all yours from 7 tonight though, I think it makes more sense to meet at the business club, the Chambers Lounge, as it will be more private and secluded from the buzz of the restaurants. I notice the boundaries in your pretty little head are shrinking a wee bit, huh?' I couldn't see him but could picture a naughty spark in his smile, smug in the knowledge that I was yielding to his charm by making a first move.

'Honey, I wouldn't bet on that. I can't tell, Z, but I do want to continue from where we left off a few days back. See you.'

'Hey beauteous! I've got good news and bad news. That I am getting hooked to your playful ways is the bad news. The good news is that by afternoon, the rupee recovered so there is some temporary cheer for now.'

'Zed, the "bad news" sounds like music to my ears…As for the "good news", rock on then! We all know when lucre is stressed, love goes on the back-burner.'

'You know, Aku, almost every time we meet, I unravel a new you. One moment, it's a Mary Antoinette at her jewellers shopping for emeralds, the next moment you are down and out with sadness, playing tragedy queen. Which is the real you?'

'Both. I am shades of grey. When I am buying emeralds, they uplift me because emeralds don't hurt! People do! On a lighter note, don't you think we are both like two psychos trying to form a connect? One's a workaholic. The other's just rebounding back to life, with boundaries in her head. I can't say each time we meet I am free of guilt. I know there are no spouses, so no one is cheating. But I am guilty of being with a younger man. Younger chronologically, though your emotional quotient seems much higher than mine, given your age. It bridges the distance, in a way.'

'Aksh, the future's not ours to see. All I know is when two beautiful minds converge, the chemistry could be magic! Let's take each day as it comes. How's that for starters? Besides, tell me, princess, when did you last set your heart free?'

'SWAK, Z! In case you don't get it, your idea is "sealed with a kiss".'

'If I am not being too audacious, tell me, Akshraa, do you fantasize?'

'Zed, what kind of question is that? Sure, I dream phantasmagorical dreams. It's only when one is six feet under that dreams die with you. If you don't dream, you can't actualize. The first blueprint of doing business or falling in love is in the realm of fantasy, isn't it? Foreplay is in the mind, dude...'

'Shall we play "fantasy-fantasy"? You tell me yours, I'll spell out mine?'

'No. In the context of your generation, I am a novice at that...I still have to learn. You could make me your protégé, if you so wish. But my generation is subtle, suggestive and not terribly articulate at foreplay. I am a wee bit shy face to face... I can write poetry or a love letter...but I don't know how to enact or talk your talk. You must think I'm quite a square, a dunce or a nun?'

'Not at all. I am raking in your old-world charm, contrasting it to the in-your-face raunchiness of a younger woman. Frankly, it's more seductive than what I see in my generation's fast-track world. The prelude to an affair is enigmatic. It's esoteric to strip through layers and layers of a woman's mind, body and soul, as the veil begins to drop subtly...A little bit of something left to the imagination... leaving any man craving for more...'

'More? ...More of what?' I asked myself nervously, not unaware where I was pushing this. What was next? Could I deal with the aftermath? It was getting too steamy to handle.

I knew it through my age and wisdom. He didn't!

Swatches of Romance with Zed

February 2015

OVER THE MONTHS, Zaheer and I had settled into a pattern, comfortable in spending time together a few days of the week. Neither of us felt a compulsive need to make each other claustrophobic by meeting every single day. The friendship matured with time, as we sometimes met up with a circle of friends and, at other times, spent time alone at each other's homes or went to see a movie.

I didn't feel serial relationships on the rebound were the answer to the void left by a marriage gone wrong. Every relationship did not have to be a full-blown romance or culminate in marriage and commitment. Romance could also be a non-physical relationship with a deep connect where two people are in sync, loving each other's company and yet not pining to be together obsessively, 24 x 7.

One freezing winter evening, we joined Zaheer's banker friends at a pub in the Delhi Golf Club. The place was buzzing with charcoal fires placed near each table as we were served piping hot kababs and tikkas grilled on an open tandoor that was built at the corner of the large terrace where we sat. Facing acres of golfing greens was a breathtakingly stunning sight as one took in a view of the contoured, manicured topography.

We had formed a circle of about eight of us, engrossed in an animated chat about the riveting fight between AAP and the BJP for the Delhi elections, the outcome of which was expected three days later. One of Lutyens' Delhi's favourite pastimes was politics. What Bollywood glamour was to Mumbai and sports was to Calcutta, politics was to Delhi. Delhi Gymkhana Club or the DGC, as well as the Delhi Golf Club, were second homes to aristocratic bureaucrats. One of the first commandments of PM Modi, when he took over the reins of governance, was that aside from babus coming to office on time they abstain from frequenting clubs. I was amused to see not one known IAS-type in sight, except for a few retired fuddy-duddies enjoying their brandy at the golf club.

At the table Meghna lamented, 'BJP playing Modi as a mascot in Maharashtra, J&K and now in Delhi is overkill. Kejriwal has reinvented his image as messiah and saviour since the last election, positioning and branding himself as the only crusader of issues from corruption to price rise. He's gaining swift ground. This is turning into a referendum on PM Modi's nine months of governance. Considering six decades of mismanagement by the Congress, I think putting him to a test so early is pretty unfair, isn't it?'

Zed chirped in, 'I am inclined to agree with you, Meghs, though a loss in the bastion of Delhi will prick the smugness of BJP's invincibility. Indians are the most fickle voters. They lived for fifty years as subjects of the Gandhis. They've suffered long enough and are now impatient to make up for lost time, punishing any ruler if he doesn't deliver soon enough.'

Modi's win just eight months back was as significant to hapless Indians in quest of a messiah to deliver them from poverty to prosperity, as was 1947 historic in the country's liberation from colonial rule.

I quipped, 'I think for now we've decided to dump Modi as the national heart-throb and romance Kejri, believing the muffler-man will pull a rabbit out of his hat. I must admit, I voted for AAP.'

'Uff! You gullible nerds!' Zaheer wasn't happy with the likely trend of results. 'You do realize that Kejriwal's leftist leanings can set Delhi back by years. Also, those nuisance satraps like Mamta's TMC, Mulayam's Samajwadi and Bihar's parties like Laloo's RJD will only get more teeth to coalesce against a party that just last year won the central elections with a landslide majority. It would be a pity if BJP loses.'

Vinay, Meghna's husband, turned towards me and said, 'I think you are right, Akshraa, when you said people are showing traces of disenchantment with Modi. The PM has frittered away his goodwill too fast, squandering his hard-earned political capital. Just read this tweet I am forwarding to you.'

It read, '@dkgdelhi: We the Maha Chutiyas of Bharat have fallen victim to the joke of 15 lakhs each in our bank account' (which was just an analogy to quantify the scale of black money, if brought back to Indian shores from Swiss accounts that Modi had promised pre-elections).

Shreya, herself a banker, said, 'Hmm, not a pretty picture, futuristically speaking. More so, it sounds bleak for us as investment strategists. The stock markets will get spooked for a while if it's an Aam Aadmi win because their egalitarian leanings border on socialism, though I do feel India is too steeped in a liberal free-market economy to regress. However, should Kejriwal win, it will be a temporary setback in the larger scheme of things.'

~

Reflections, as I leap-frog and cut to 2016...

A year after the Modi loss and Kejriwal win in Delhi, it was perceived that Gulliver had lost to Lilliput, and not that the BJP had lost to AAP. Kejriwal, the outsider, had upstaged the newest incumbent to Lutyens' seat of power, as BJP, the mainstream party, was challenged on its home turf in the Union Territory of Delhi by a regional newcomer, too soon for comfort. Modi, himself the outsider to central politics, was now threatened by Kejriwal, the bureaucrat-turned-messiah, a 'political guerrilla', a novice to politics, though not to administration. Both contenders had understood the political marketplace well by branding themselves as messiahs of change to deliver a new kind of politics to Indians, who yearned to dislodge a system corroded with corruption and Dosco-Ivy League aristocrats that had governed for forty-nine of the sixty-eight years since Independence.

As I wrote in April 2016, it was just two years back that Modi had stormed the bastion and smugness of the ruling elite in Delhi with his ascension. The debacle of winning just three seats and losing sixty-seven in the Delhi state elections was too soon, just seven months after Modi's meteoric win at the centre, to sense a reversal of tide which left much for BJP to introspect after the Delhi defeat.

Was Modi's appeal on the wane or had he over-committed and underperformed on his promise of 'achhe din'? Or was it a restive public that was impatient for change within just seven months of NDA that wanted to give Modi a message that there was a political niche vacant for an alternative maverick if he did not deliver soon enough?

The role of Atal Bihari Vajpayee, the political elder and forefather of the party, had begun to resurface in public debate and dialogue, his tenure being perceived as perhaps larger than it was in hindsight, as the Modi-era was getting on to be two years old. Comparisons are odious, but they were happening. Was Vajpayee's statesman-like sobriety being over-glorified by the media in contrast to Modi's brashness and overdrive?

Modi, the master strategist, had pre-empted the shelf-life of the mandir politics of the last era and sought to match up to Atalji by toning down Hindutva way back in his pre-electoral oratory. He had astutely self-corrected the fault-lines of the previous BJP regime, realizing it would not take him or his brand appeal too far in India or a globalized world unless he kept his focus on resurrecting BJPs previous manifesto of an 'India Shining' economic agenda.

Travelling to far corners of the world in search of investments, Modi took upon himself the role of CEO of the country in order to raise the equity of Brand India and Brand Modi. The PM in his silent wisdom had decided that religious fervour was the drumbeat of the last century, and this decade was all about youth, jobs, money, prosperity and good economics. So he kept his ideological parent, the RSS, happy, yet did his own thing. He allowed himself the luxury to play 'good cop' by letting the rabid Yogi Adityanaths and Baba Ramdevs play 'bad cop', by never chiding their hyper-nationalism and 'off-with-their-heads' oratory. With Ramdev's jingoism that Indians who refused to kowtow to the chants of 'Bharat Mata ki Jai' were best beheaded, the Baba kept alive the appeal of Hindu fascists amidst raging student debates as to who is deemed seditious and who is anti-India, or really: who is anti-Hindu?

So by 2016, Modi had it both ways by keeping the rabble-rouser motormouths of the RSS happy, yet focusing on delivering 'achhe din', however remote it seems nearly mid-way through his rule.

However, the striking contrast from UPA II, and the similarities of two years into Modi's rule and one year into Kejriwal's rule at the centre is that till now, fortunately, Lutyens' power elite are at bay... Completely sanitized from fixers, and fortunately with no known citings of 'coteries' in the offing till date!

~

We sat in the car and neither of us really wanted to end the evening at eleven. It was late enough, though not quite, so we decided to enjoy a cappuccino at the Taj. Suddenly, from the chat on politics at the club, Zaheer changed the conversation, as a touch of his hand made my pulse react, intoning, 'Aksh, do you love me?'

Silence…

'I asked you a question, Akshu!'

'I kind of do…Zed,' I said gently.

'That's like saying I am half-pregnant, Akshraa! What do I make of this vague answer?'

'Because I measure my words… That I am, as of now, like in Chetan Bhagat's book, your half-girlfriend… that I have one foot into us and one foot in the stream of life. Cruising, you could say, in a feeling of nowhereness… drifting without a destination, for now,' I explained. 'Zed, please pass me that paper napkin by your side as I've smudged mine with my lipstick.' On which I proceeded to scribble the answer that came from my heart, too shy to articulate what my smile betrayed. 'Zed, you take my breath away. I am crazy about you…allow me the luxury of time, please?'

He looked deep into my eyes with an evaluating gaze, relieved, I thought a bit presumptuously, that his feelings of love were being reciprocated. But deceptively, my heart ached with reminiscing flashes of the beginnings of romance with Surya two decades back. I was filled with the guilt of being disloyal to a man I logically owed no loyalty to, flushed with a bit of shame at gravitating towards Zaheer.

~

The following evening I called Zed around 6 p.m. 'Zed, I want to speak to you and place my heavily laden thoughts on your broad shoulders. Can we do dinner at my house tonight?'

'Not before 9.30 p.m., Aksh. I might even be later than that. I am at the BlackRock India Investors' Summit, where I want to know what the global view of asset managers is and their strategies in the run-up to the budget are. I need to get a pulse on how FIIs are viewing the India story post-Modi. It's boring stuff for you but it's important for me to know what is the view of my peers in the banking world. Will you grant me some leeway if I am late?'

He arrived in a dapper black business suit that contrasted well with a sharp canary-yellow tie, his hair dishevelled after a long day at work, yet full of bouncy energy. 'May I take the liberty of fixing my first drink, please? I like my first whiskey stiff so I am in sync with your thoughts, my beauteous.'

'Sure, what's mine is yours...don't be my guest, be my host too. Make the same for me, please. By the way, you are looking swell in this suit. Ever occur to you that you could become a cool cat by aping PM Modi's sartorial style by getting yourself a monogramed Savile Row suit with your initials imprinted all the way down to your shoes?' I joked as I coquettishly tugged his tie towards me.

~

We finished dinner but I was hesitant about belling the cat and getting to the issue I wanted to address. It was past midnight when Zaheer asked, 'Tell me what's on your mind, Aku? You've never since the time I've known you ever cared to meet twice in the same day. Honey, is it your love or your lust that called me this evening?'

I gulped a few sips nervously as I replied, 'Zed, when I feel good and strong and uncluttered from the burden of my past, when I am ready to be in the real world again, I will open my heart to you and you alone. I have found love again maybe too soon after my break-up. But to paraphrase Elizabeth Gilbert in *Eat, Pray, Love*, never ever do I want to use another person's body or emotions as a scratching post for my own unfulfilled yearnings. Will you allow me the luxury to return to you someday, to come back to you in a more meaningful and authentic version of myself?'

His expression changed instantly, hurt writ all over his face.

'I am disappointed, Aksh! Is this what we are here to discuss? Get this straight: you are not using me. We haven't even consummated this relationship and yet you feel like you are guilty of betraying a man who hurt you for over two decades! Why can't you give yourself and me a chance to let this mature into something meaningful, without being haunted by your past?'

'Because you are much younger than me. I don't want to rob you of precious time should you come across a good woman with whom you could one day settle down, who will bear you children and complete your world. What's in it for you, honey, if we ever did have a future? A few good years? Maybe as I talk, it's an awakening for me too, a serious one at that, in coming to terms with my own mortality. Honestly, I don't want to be selfish.'

'What if I tell you I've thought this through? It's a sacrifice I am willing to make to own you for the rest of my life even if it means no children.' My heart reached out to his innocent subjugation. I loved it and hated myself in equal measure.

'My conscience would kill me. Besides, I would hate these society cats gossiping behind our backs and saying, "Now Akshraa Mittal has trapped a toy boy!" A few years from now, our age difference could tell on you more than on me.'

'I'll tell you what, Akshraa, let's just leave this at status quo. Let us ride this out for a little while more…cherish the moment without second-guessing what tomorrow holds.'

'But no deadlines, Zed, promise? No pressures on either side, sweetie?' I requested.

Zed was gracious enough to give us a breather, a pause where I could have the best of my new-found independence and savour his companionship too. I needed to sort out my mind and morals with time unbound.

Goa with Zed, and the Mittal Flashback

June 2015

WE MADE AN unplanned weekend getaway to Goa in June, luxuriating in an escape to a make-believe world. Zaheer decided to subtly play shrink to my wayward, wild and wavering mind, considering it should have been the other way around. His maturity confounded as did his caressing ardour.

Staying in separate rooms drew boundaries for now. It was partly my convent prudishness at play but his youthful lightness let it pass, assuming it to be some mid-age idiosyncrasy of an older woman. This age group gave little thought to trivia of this kind.

I felt a huge surge of upliftment, one that comes when you sense someone believes in you, the very opposite of humiliation. Besides, there was an unmistakable spirited joie de vivre amongst Punjabis in their effervescence and passion for living it up, so I loved being with someone of my ilk and from my land, feeling a warm comfort in the familiarity of my own community. Comparisons are odious, yet I couldn't help contrast Zed's earthiness with Surya's feudal ways that spoke down to me with arrogance. If Zaheer overwhelmed me, I felt underwhelmed when belittled by Surya.

We had requested The Leela's manager to set up a table by the sea. Over a dinner of foie gras by the beach, he uncorked a Moet & Chandon's, which was a Rosé Imperial Tie Coffret champagne. A soft pink bubbly, tinted in amber and aged over two years, its intense bouquet was a toast to a mellowing dusk.

In the early stages of a relationship, there's a certain something that's tantalizing and seductive in knowing that one day, it would or could consummate into something sensuous and wholesome. Those guessing games adults play! Not your one-night stands that the young and restless enact. This was adult footsie! He knew it. I knew it.

During the two nights we spent at the resort, he was curious about the kind of man Surya was and a bit about the life I lived with him. Was he sizing me up to fathom if I was a high-maintenance social titli, a richie-rich butterfly whom he would have to painfully live up to? But I must admit he heard me out indulgently without the accompanying emotions of jealousy a man or woman display when an ex-spouse is discussed.

'This was a kattar Hindutva kind of family, Zed,' I began. 'They were unapologetically unsecular, ideologically in favour of deporting the last remnants of minorities should they come in the way of building a temple at Ayodhya. With the resurgence of Hindu pride, I dare say, there was a sect in our country who would have secretly wished to lay siege over any or every ancient mosque and build a temple over it, claiming it was once the abode of one of our thousand Hindu gods or goddesses. The Mittals epitomized the repressed spirit of "garv" that was burning in every Hindu heart.'

He interrupted me, 'By nature, we Hindus are passive warriors, not zealots unlike some rabid sects, when it comes to reclamation of our rights. I don't think most Indian homes are that obsessed with religion, or are they? So much of religion must have been oppressive, I'd imagine? I could have been asphyxiated by such hardcore theism!'

'Yes. It was rigid!' I said. 'So devout, don't laugh, that Surya strictly adhered to abstinence during navratras. The body language was clear, "No sex please, we are purists", conveniently forgetting that we hail from the land of Kamasutra! Anyway, jokes apart, it was a prevalent belief that we should not have sworn to a secular constitution at the time we gained independence. This is a strain of thought that I am seeing re-emerging since Modi became PM. Shifting from the modernist, secular world I grew up in, educated by "missionary" nuns in Loreto Convent, to this new-found revivalism and pride in Hindutva, wasn't difficult but yet it felt strange to reconcile the two worlds. With the passage of years, I sadly-happily merged into the Mittal identity, thinking, behaving, eating and talking like them. Today, I am proud of it. Earlier, I was awkward. I found this extreme patriotism, nationalism and tradition a bit too restrictive. Sometimes even irritating!'

'Nothing flawed in that, Aksh,' he smiled. 'Many elders, including my grandparents, believed India's freedom from colonial rule in 1948 was a lie, fed to gullible people by Nehru, "a dog of capitalism". In a way, they condemned Nehru for not having made India a near-theocratic state like its neighbours. Now, the point is, my generation is different. The Partition, Ayodhya, the riots of 1984 or even the Gujarat 2002 massacre… Who cares? The average age group of most of India, of almost 65 per cent of the country is thirty-five. They weren't even born when these events occurred or most were in their infancy. Those periods can be googled or Wikipediaed. They would have only learned it in a history class. So how remote is an emotional experience when you have never lived through it? It's so last century, for God's sake! What really matters to people in their twenties, thirties and forties is the economy, prosperity, jobs, meritocracy and a good quality of life, Aksh. The youth reject the moral policing of the divisive Hindutva brigade, for example, like trying to push the Bhagwad Gita as our national scripture or banning beef. Religion is a matter of private belief. Being liberal is a mindset, wouldn't you agree? Anyway,' he continued, 'you sure lived the life of a princess. Has the stupor waned after so many years of estrangement?'

I sighed. 'Yes, the stupor has waned, Zaheer, but memories never die! I live in the present; yet, when I think back it's like a déjà vu to see of how business history repeated itself within the Mittal family. I relive stories Surya used to recount of his grandfather's heydays as equally of his blunders. The founder of the Mittal empire, he owned three palatial houses in the limited territory of Lutyens' Delhi, gifting one house to each of the wives he married, a sprawling 2 acres each. Of course, the luxury he conferred on each wife was never equal, as his largesse varied with his moods, as to who was the preferred choice in being the wife of the day! Suryaprakash acquired the fourth house, with the success of his own business aptitude, to add to the privileged fleet of addresses.

'Now Zaheer, Nehru, known to be agnostic, was averse to Mittal, who owned one of the biggest Indian business houses of those times, for being an avid supporter of the Hindu lobby within the Congress. Ultimately, the government of the day succeeded in framing Mittal on alleged wrongdoings within his companies and decimating his empire, a price he paid for opposing political heavyweights of those times. Nearly five decades later, I am privy to Surya repeating history. It seems like an encore of his grandfather's business blunders. Dada ji had investments across sectors, from cement, steel and textiles and coal to media, even a township in Odisha named after him, Mittalnagar. But each and every business was brought to ground zero. I was told by one of his daughters that at a karmic level, his downfall was attributed to a strong belief that men who do not accord respect to the women of the house incur the wrath of Goddess Laxmi.'

I continued, 'Surya, too, diversified recklessly without consolidating and took on powerful politicians. I think wise business czars don't publicly align with any political party or go anti-establishment. It's a strategy inimical to the growth of any vibrant empire.'

'Does it embitter you, Akshraa?' Zed asked. 'You've been through highs and troughs probably more turbulent than the ocean waves we are sitting in front of.'

'What is swept with the tide has gone, Zaheer...,' I said, gazing at the sea. 'It merged into the infinity of nothingness. Trust me, if ever we share a future, the one thing I want you to know is that my story with Surya ended a long time back. Tell me, Z, what's your scene with your wife Chitra? Why did you split?'

He paused and then answered, 'Chitra was very beautiful. She was from one of the lesser-known royal families of Rajgarh. They were not terribly affluent but extremely comfortable. I was a struggling executive when we met. She was reasonably well educated but was an alcoholic. She would start from 5 in the evening, so by the time I would get home after 7, she was sozzled. It's something she very adeptly hid from me for the six months that we were engaged. I felt her parents had a hint of her addiction but never revealed anything about it, keen to get her married in her early twenties. I succeeded in getting her partially cured after putting her in rehab for some months. But that initial romance or any feelings I had were repulsed at seeing a woman inebriated each evening. I had a career ahead and wanted to make something of my life. I couldn't have built my world around a woman like her nor taken my life forward in a meaningful way. Fortunately she did not oppose the divorce, so it was a short-lived marriage. The few passing encounters I had thereafter were with productive, working, thinking women. At least while dating them, there was a mental connect! Akshraa, is a man meant to be beholden to a woman just for her looks? Beauty wasn't enough to sustain my interest in her. I was on track to grow in my job. I was hugely driven. I wasn't about to let a bad marriage come in the way of my ambitious goals. Today, I have found a woman of substance in you. We talk and connect at multiple levels with each other. I would do anything to get you into my world. Maybe I can't offer you a lifestyle of the rich and famous that you were used to with Surya. But I can offer you a future in earnestness, where I hope you would never have to revisit your painful past.'

He continued, 'I did tell you I am commitment-phobic when I met you on our first date. That's because I wanted to get to the top of my job. I can't afford the luxury of getting derailed again. But I think we are in sync, aside from the fiery chemistry we share. At forty-seven, I am also coming to terms with the brevity of lifespans. YOLO—you only live once! I am keen to build a relationship with you, having had a non-existent one before.'

❧

We chatted a lot those two days and nights, taking moonlit strolls by the beach, listening to music, swimming and getting massages in the afternoons. There was a languorous tempo to those few days. The wafting aroma of jasmine after a massage lingered in the room and on my body as we lazed in the verandah till the twilight hour. Secretly, questions clamoured for answers. We tried skirting around them. Neither of us was in a hurry to shake off the charade and confront uneasy truths.

Part V

Just How Many Endings Does One Traverse in a Lifetime?

How Many Farewells are We Ordained to Endure in One Life?

19 June 2015

THE HEART HAS had its yearnings, destiny its pulls. We never do know which of them eventually trumps!

Abruptly and sadly, Zaheer and I never saw each other ever again. I can't say I was untouched by the disconnect. Not even the boundaries I had put on myself and him, of keeping the relationship at 'a little more than friendship, a little less than an affair', were possible to play out. I hoped I would get a chance someday to explain the circumstances that must have made me come across as callous, inconsistent and uncaring. To board a flight of fantasy on a whim to Goa and then to disappear after such an intense emotional experience must have made him think I was flippant. He tried to reach me a few times till pride must have made him refrain from the outreach. I just stopped taking his calls or replying to his messages.

This happened because something more serious had transpired, more dire and dismal than I had ever imagined. Ominously, my worst fears manifested as despondency gripped me.

Surya had been imprisoned.

That overtook all other emotions.

Estranged for so many years from Surya, we were already severed and far apart. How much further was he now going to be from me, where I would never have access to him even if I ever craved to hear his voice?

I was broken this time, to put it mildly.

~

Day of Reckoning

How I wished the news was a lie. That this was not my affliction but an eerie occurrence striking someone whom I did not know in a remote corner of the world.

Logically, I should have been indifferent.

But Suryaprakash's time in jail was testing my integrity as a person. I found it hard to turn my back on someone I had shared a lifetime with, as though it all never happened.

When finally my Day of Judgment came, would it then be ordained for me, 'To deepest hell, highest heaven or back to earth again?' The soul of man weeps in grief if it cannot redeem its pledge to itself, creating a painful cycle of life after life only to reincarnate in order to fulfil its deepest yearnings.

Personally, I rejected the fatalism of Hindu inculcation of past-life karma as being the cause of sufferance in this life, as also disbelieved in life after death. However, should there be a next life, I needed to complete the give and take of my karmic cycle in this lifetime, whatever it took to achieve deliverance from my bond with Surya. The life I lived with him—good, bad or ugly—needed to end with this birth. If it were within the realm of a mortal to expiate in the here and now of this life cycle, I needed to do so in order to not carry forward that burden into the reincarnation of life after life.

Quite honestly, one life of suffering was enough. But I was endlessly pained by the self-created destruction he had wrought upon himself. It was unnecessary and could have been averted.

As in a Greek tragedy, when god wills a nemesis, he first destroys the mind of man so he makes fatal errors of judgment that bring self-inflicted misery.

Easy Money like a Falling Star, the Fall and Fall of Indian Czars

May 2015

AS GEORGE ORWELL once said philosophically, whoever is winning at the moment will always seem to be invincible. That's what Indian business mandarins felt in the period from 2003 to 2008 when the world and the Indian economy were thriving.

The Indian economy had begun to appear increasingly rigged by the end of the UPA-II regime, as big business houses had doubled spends on government and lobbying in return for favours. During the heady years of UPA I, entrepreneurs rashly ventured into areas unrelated to their core competencies. They went on a rampage of mergers and acquisitions to lay siege to distressed assets and companies and to grow their empires on leveraged funding in order to diversify. Banks were flushed with funds, recklessly lending money to finance these expansions. If money couldn't be raised domestically, there was the option of foreign funding, where money could be raised internationally by issuing foreign currency convertible bonds (FCCBs) for which the rate of interest was almost close to zero.

But once the global meltdown struck and demand slackened, the debts of the largest business houses mounted, necessitating the sale of prime assets to square off borrowings. The biggest-ever sale of corporate assets in Indian history had begun, as the so-called 'suited-booted sarkar' began to clamp down on corporates that had had a free run with borrowing easy money from banks during Congress rule to procure assets for themselves. To square off debts, they were being forced to liquidate their stakes within the listed companies as also prime land, rental and capital assets at distressed prices, whether it was Vijay Mallya or the Sahara Group.

It was a carnage that affected the asset quality of banks, due to slackening demand that affected aviation, infrastructure, commodities, exports and real-estate industries. Perhaps the only sectors that were relatively insulated were pharmaceuticals, healthcare and the services sector.

However, this did not mean that all of industry could be painted with the same brush. There were genuine cases of default due to a reversal of business cycles, like Tata Corus, or due to cost and time overruns in infrastructure segments. The nature and cause of Suryaprakash's losses was more in line with the latter companies that were victims of the business cycle. So they could not be deemed wilful defaulters.

~

Suryaprakash was an oddball. Few are born with a platinum spoon studded with diamonds, but as he gained fame and fortune, he fumbled and erred on the wrong side of people and destiny. When you are born a king and perceived as a demigod, you have to be maniacally self-destructive to fling your fate into Satan's grip. Despite being a scion of a deeply religious family, aberrations can make you skid down the highway to hell!

When I was younger, I had seen him reign imperiously,

holding court with the might of a king over his turf and his minions. He was ahead of the curve in the 1980s, buying out politicians like pups, throwing crumbs at them and striking sweetheart business deals.

But by 1991, like his industrial peers, Surya too had to play 'catch-up', as in the global game of business, the dice rolled faster than his grasp. Old ways of business were untenable in a modernist world. He unwittingly got into the hands of loan and land sharks. It was difficult to fathom what led him to dig his hole in a prison cell when he had the choice of negotiating an honourable exit!

Compromise was alien to his rigid nature, as he never knew what meeting anyone midway meant, with man, woman or business associate. Born to win, never knowing what the subjugation of a loser felt, was a trait I attributed to some childhood dysfunctionality. It was like when elders never correct errant or prodigal children. Might is right, and powerplay a fun tool in a chimp's hands.

Yerawada Jail, Pune

July 2015

WHEN BUSINESS CHANNELS CNBC, NDTV Profit, etc. blazed 'Breaking News' stories showing humiliating images of Surya appearing before the Economic Offences Wing and being detained, I cried like a baby. From a habitat in the majestic environs of Lutyens' Delhi, living on acres of stately land, a man of valour and might had chosen to languish in a morbid prison cell within the confines of Yerawada Jail in Pune and habitate amongst petty criminals. Death wish, maybe? It compelled me to deliberate: did Surya at a deeper level prefer the hellhole of imprisonment to the hellish conditions he had created in his life in the outside world? Or was it his stubborn, unyielding nature not to strike a compromise at any cost?

When Surya was in jail, I wanted to go and meet him and maybe give him a warm hug, despite the barriers that remained between us, physical and emotional. I visualized meeting him through iron bars dividing us, where hearts might speak but a physical embrace could not consummate. But I failed to draw upon my reservoirs of strength to revive or relive that proximity.

My conscience implored me to visit him but my mind negated that calling. In that tug-of-war in my head, I was frozen in inaction as an escapist wanting to distance myself from the inconvenient crisis at hand.

But life was about confronting uncomfortable truths. This trial was his. This test was his. This karma was his. But this dark hour was not his alone. I had shared the good times and I couldn't walk away from the worst times. This was equally my moment of reckoning, my unfinished karma. We had spent a lifetime together. We both had to transcend this difficult phase individually and subsequently face the post-prison trauma that was bound to ensue. We were, however, constantly in touch as I wrote to him frequently, my brief notes sent to his secretary who conveyed back his messages on a nearly daily basis.

I was too feeble-hearted to face reality, so I initially googled Yerawada Jail in Pune. My hair stood on end as I was spooked on reading about the appalling living conditions of the inmates there. Here I was sitting in the luxury of my air-conditioned suite, while he must be sweltering in the heat of Pune's humid July with possibly just a dust-laden fan swirling hot air within the cubicle. I Googled the routine of the inmates which gave me an idea of their typical day. They were to awaken by 5 a.m., followed by breakfast at 7.30 a.m., after which they engaged in carpentry, leather work or tailoring, or spent time in the library. Then was lunch at 11.30 a.m., after which they resumed their activities that continued till 4.30, returning to their cells by 7 p.m.

Who in their rational sense would opt for such a life, when they had the choice to negotiate with their petitioner?

'Dear Lord, your tests are too hard. Can you be just a little less harsh? If only just occasionally?' I implored.

Games People Played

September 2015

ARVIND, SURYA'S COUSIN brother, had been trying to wrest control of MCL while he was imprisoned. He had been inducted into Surya's business when he had completed his graduation. As the age difference between Surya and Arvind was eighteen years, Surya treated him as a son as the joint family was very close knit, besides there being no other male member within the family to induct into his growing empire. With the passage of time and a feeling of trust in Arvind, Surya conferred on him a generous 25 per cent equity in the holding company. Surya's sisters owned the rest, though they were not allowed nor had a desire to have an active role in business. Arvind was not bright, but extremely hard-working and loyal, so Surya felt his faith in him was not misplaced, and being given the largesse of equity by his elder brother, he was sure to remain eternally beholden to him. Arvind grew in stature and experience, gradually being given greater decision-making powers within the conglomerate, much to the displeasure of Surya's two sisters who felt threatened with Arvind gaining stature and their elder brother's complete confidence.

Arvind had a predilection for the finer things of life, though Surya always told me he had no contribution towards earning his pleasures, being a dunce who lived off reflected glory and riches. He was in it only for the good times.

Over family dinners, my favourite pastime was to pick on the moron, though he hadn't a clue that he was my amusement for the evening. Any cerebral topic veered back to the finest luxury hotels of the world, the smoothest cigars or the best airline to travel first-class. Or the topic would skid to the best chicks in town, the finest champagne or the latest cars to hit the market. A trend rampant amongst political and business dynasties in India was the right to ascend, regardless of competence or meritocracy. Corporate battles in India between father and son or siblings were playing out in the backyards of nearly every business family. Revenge was the strongest motive that triggered feuds and divided families, as sinister ambition knew no boundaries in business or politics.

Another mastermind in this drama was Ramesh Yadav, a politician, who had a stake in a healthcare company that Surya had allegedly defaulted with. Surya, in his heyday twenty years ago, had, in his utter arrogance, treated Ramesh Yadav like a minion. It was a humiliation Yadav was out to avenge, aside from his covert business interest being at stake in the land deal through proxy holdings.

How on earth did he have the resources to own a stake in a healthcare company in the first place? Years of Yadav's demonic might had plagued the state with misrule. This man was infamous for food scarcity, inflated prices of grains, land grabbing, farmer suicides and venality of every form during his tenure in Bihar, an epitome of the rot that prevailed in our political system. I had decided to forget my estrangement with Surya, absolving him of the past and motivating myself to show my mettle by taking this fight to the boardroom. 'Only few people are brilliant. What if you are not? If you can't beat them at their game, try to change the game itself.' I loved this attitude, which became my template for strategizing.

My vengefulness was now directed towards putting up a joint fight. I hoped this fight would lead me right up to Arvind's doorstep. I was adamant to foil his evil designs and the power games he was playing during his elder brother's absence. Wrong was wrong. But then, don't cowards always try to manipulate and prey on the weak?

I was to talk to the best lawyers and chartered accountants to fight for Surya's diminishing rights and try to retrieve his waning powers in absentia by educating myself about my own privileges as a minuscule stakeholder and asserting them. If needed, I would gather the forces to oppose any resolution the company passed that might be remotely averse to Surya. I was on Surya's side without a doubt. In his hour of need, it was imperative that I get a power of attorney or assert my shareholding rights as this was too unequal a fight to usurp his rights.

I had collected startling facts of multiple intrigues that were at play to destroy Surya and the empire that he had diligently built in his thirties. For one, Arvind and his loyalists had begun to pilfer money through purchases and convert profits into losses so as to siphon out cash. His company inflated the value of raw materials imported from Indonesia and siphoned money abroad. He would pay the actual supplier the cost of the material, while the balance was routed through his partnership firms via Dubai. Second, the giant healthcare company which was behind his imprisonment, complicit with the devilish Ramesh Yadav, had decided to further pressure Surya by buying into the shares of MCL in order to dilute Surya's holdings and supremacy in the cement company, while he was imprisoned and helpless.

MCL's share price on the stock exchange had languished at

₹17 for the last two years, never managing to reach the peak of ₹327 that it was at before the economic downturn. There was a sustained and gradual spike, like a creeping acquisition, that drove the stock price from ₹17 to ₹131, an abnormal jump, as they tried to augment their ownership and increase their holdings within the company.

Though Ramesh Yadav's party, the Indian National Samajik Party (INSP), had lost the elections, they proceeded to offer support to a minority government with the devious intent to piggyback to power, or at least avert an inquiry into disproportionate assets cases pending against most MLAs and ex-ministers of the party. When you strip a politician in India who has reigned for decades lording over the land mafia, he is a wounded lion. The lion wanted blood! Blood of humans and blood of weaker sections of society to prey on. And blood money? That's even more delicious for a savage beast to devour. Foolishly, Suryaprakash believed his time in jail was worth a few months of hardship to tide the crisis and await the defeat of his predator, as most of the national polls had predicted a thumping majority for Yadav's opponents. He believed that a few months of tough times in prison would help him avenge his rights and turn the tide back in his favour as by then, Yadav would be powerless post an electoral debacle. Sadly, Ramesh Yadav still held the reins of power from behind the scenes despite his minority in the state legislature. Despite Yadav being a heavyweight politician from Bihar, his sphere of influence extended to a complete control over the courts and police authorities even in Maharashtra, and ensured Surya's attempts at securing bail failed as he had turned it into an ego battle. Ramesh also stood to gain a few hundred crores if the healthcare company won the litigation. Though it was petty cash for someone who was estimated to be worth some whopping ₹7,000 crore, it was Yadav's arrogance as much as his avaricious greed at stake.

Surya's misplaced optimism made him foolishly clutch at straws. His opponents, political as well as business, including his younger brother, were gaining ground steadily. The latter, who was timid as a squirrel in his elder brother's presence, was now nibbling at the cheese, creaming the company with his own set of chamchas. This was kalyug, a contrast to Bharat, Lord Ram's faithful brother, who kept the throne of Ayodhya vacant and venerated the khadaus (slippers) of his elder brother till his return from exile.

Life's Hard; It's Even Harder When You're Stupid

ANJALI FLEW DOWN from Calcutta to see me through those days. She was my oldest friend, my critic and my mentor who helped me form an achievable strategy to safeguard Surya's interests. We discussed the pros and cons in great detail, arguing and brainstorming a strategy for a way forward.

'Firstly, Akshraa, you need to be unfazed by Surya's opponents and not be intimidated by their strength in numbers, or their financial staying power. Arvind's game plan is to gather a lynch mob within the large House of Mittals to financially slay his elder brother when and if he is freed. Remember, David won against Goliath because he evolved a smart strategy by using Goliath's weaknesses to his vantage. You have to stay strong and have the wherewithal for a fight that could be of a long duration,' she said. 'Secondly, you need to know how Arvind is messing up the company affairs, and where and if he is goofing up. For that, you definitely need one of his key people on your side. An infallible strategy is, "Never interrupt your enemy when he is making a mistake."'

'Anjali, I have in the past few days managed to network with some of the minority shareholders to have a meeting with them and apprise them of Arvind's manipulation of the books of account. Let's not forget, he only knows the gaddi culture way of doing business and pulling out cash. I have come to know a lot of underhanded dealings from Venkataraman, Arvind's secretary, as I've now got him on my payroll. He says Arvind has been over-invoicing on shipments. He's been using shareholder funds to support his extravagant lifestyle. He has formed shell companies, using those firms for mega business deals that are gradually building up cash on their books through money taken out of the public limited MCL. He is making loads of cash through purchases of raw material. Now this could be deemed an act of impropriety as he is defrauding investors. With the accrual, he is busy buying out parcels of agricultural land from hapless farmers, complicit with government officials in the neighbouring state, being close to the CM. His ultimate game plan is to tweak the rules and get government permissions for agricultural land to be converted to residential or commercial use. He obviously then rakes in windfall personal gains from the thousands of acres he has acquired for a song.' I continued, 'This will yield supernatural personal profits away from a company listed on the stock exchange, beyond the control of the Securities and Exchange Board of India, giving them no teeth to bite into his lucrative deals. If proved, though, he could be convicted for misappropriation of investor funds as also debarred from the stock exchange. I need to establish the validity of these facts before proceeding against him by having substantial proof to nail his nefarious dealings.'

Anjali was measured in her response. 'For this you need the shareholders on your side. The way forward is to strike at his misdemeanours, enlighten the stakeholders and prove that these shell companies are where the stealth wealth of MCL is parked, and that he is growing his parallel empire through this vertical.

I'm not sure it's going to be easy to nail Arvind, my dear.'

'Wowsie! Anjali, I am utterly excited at the thought of one day seeing Arvind framed and put behind bars. To go and visit him like a monkey in a cage, taking peanuts to offer him, is my ultimate dream. A sweet fantasy! I hope it happens sooner than later,' I told her. 'Meanwhile, Anjali, for the lighter side of life, Sanjay Dutt is also in the same prison, I think. I wonder if Surya has gotten to be friends with him?' I laughed.

People dreamt big; I dreamt small!

Sweet Revenge

BY AMENDING CORPORATE regulations, the Securities and Exchange Board of India (SEBI) was empowering the small-time shareholder by giving him teeth to assert himself and also tightening its vigilant watch over the inner workings of companies. When an investor deployed his hard-earned money to own a stake in the shares of a firm, this gave him a legitimate right to vote for or against certain managerial decisions before they were passed and implemented by the board. In effect, that made the smallest shareholder also an owner of the business he had bought into. SEBI guidelines of the Companies Act of 2013 did not allow promoters or controlling shareholders to vote on transactions in which they had a vested interest. As a result, the retail investor had vetoing rights.

Consequently, a gamut of decisions from board appointments, sale of business, creation of mortgage assets or reappointment of a promoter, lay with the retail investor, and the management could be compelled to withdraw a policy inimical to the interest of the investor.

Arvind had appointed his twenty-four-year-old son, who was a bigger dunce than his father, on the board. His hobby was playing games like Angry Birds on his smartphone during meetings, comprehending little or nothing of what was being discussed. Arvind's remuneration was a hefty ₹18 crore a year, completely disproportionate to MCL's earnings or net profits. How had he awarded himself this largesse?

Then there was a huge surplus land parcel of 467 acres near Jaipur in Rajasthan that was a real-estate asset belonging to the public-listed MCL that he was planning to offer as collateral in order to take a loan to develop his own business in UP. He was clearly carving assets or money out of the public-listed MCL and putting it in his privately owned company, Krishna Estate. The ownership of this company was held by his wife, two daughters and son. How was he getting away with corporate fraud on shareholders' money?

I was coming closer to my goals of nailing Arvind's opaque ways of functioning, gathering circumstantial evidence in order to build up a case for shareholders to assert their rights.

The next board meeting was scheduled in ten days, though Surya's bail hearing had been postponed by three weeks. That gave Arvind enough room to implement his devious designs in case Don, as they referred to Surya in code, was released. Don would predictably go on a rampage to quash Arvind's plans, if he was released from jail before the board meeting.

For whatever had to be done, time was of the essence. Equally, the clock was ticking to get a majority of the shareholders to vote out his resolutions.

I was playing to win…if not to win, at least to stymie Arvind's plans.

I held three rounds of meetings with shareholders, both minority retail investors and financial institutions, to adequately apprise as well as incite their fury to vote against giving their approval on a series of special resolutions at the extraordinary general meeting. Eventually, they rejected eight of the ten approvals that MCL's board was trying to get passed, including the collateral of the land parcel in Rajasthan.

To gain approvals, 75 per cent of the total votes polled by shareholders had to be in favour of the resolution. Eight fell short of the mark and that came as a body blow to Arvind's strategies.

Any shareholder holding over 10 per cent of the total equity capital could convene an extraordinary general meeting to remove the top management or question corporate decisions. I had gotten to know one Govardhan Patel, a Calcutta broker who owned a sizeable portion of the shares, and apprised him on issues of misgovernance. At the EGM that was subsequently held, Patel complained that the board of directors had failed to disclose critical information reflecting the poor standards of corporate governance at MCL.

Arvind, by now, knew who was behind his designs being checkmated. After having achieved my limited goal of obstructing his path, I let go. I wasn't concerned about the intricate workings of the company after that.

Revenge has been the strongest motive that triggered historic wars and corporate feuds through the ages. The most contentious issues that involved man being harmed by man, or divided woman from man or child, were love, lucre or territorial rights. Pernicious greed and sinister ambition knew no morality or boundaries of decency. So may I be forgiven for my evil compulsions as being only humbly, human?

⁓

At the conclusion of this battle, Anjali said to me, 'Even in the Bhagwad Gita, Lord Krishna had exhorted Arjuna the warrior into a combat he did not seek. He was guided to accept the circumstances with equanimity and to fulfil his role with honour, without grieving at loss of life or the sorrow that ensued from the tragedy.'

Awaiting Surya's Homecoming. But to which Home?

November 2015

A SEASON HAD lapsed. The sweltering heat and dust of Delhi's summer had given way to a muggy monsoon that had come and gone. There still seemed no immediate signs of Surya's release. The season of love was setting in, heralding its arrival with chrysanthemums in resplendent colours of crimson, aubergine, white and sunlight yellow. We both tended to measure lifespans in terms of winters left to live through. It was just such a festive four months of the year in the capital.

In happier climes and times, we had lounged at the patio with sigris containing charcoal and wood. The mellow outdoor lighting looked like a quaint hill station, each lamp encircled by a silvery glow of mist and fog. We listened to mellifluous sufi music, relishing my cider apple and cinnamon wine as Surya sipped his Chardonnay in a tall stemmed glass, dipping into a flaming fondue, whiling away the hours till dinner was laid.

Each time I heard news through intermediaries that Surya stood a fair chance of being granted bail, I would wonder just how would we greet each other again? In a way, I was meeting an old love but in a new mould. Like a bride on her wedding night, I was confused and exhilarated as I wondered which saree to wear. Would he even notice how I looked? Would he be loving, or formal and distant, on our first meeting? It almost felt like a blind date. Should I ask him if he had made friends in jail? Dumb idea! On second thought, that was absurd, lest he thought I was ridiculing his term in prison. I couldn't make him revisit that painful period! Wrong opening line. Gosh, was I rehearsing for a play and getting my lines all wrong due to cold feet!

Then what initiating conversation does one make? What pleasantries does one exchange, as I was hardly talking to someone who had just returned after a pleasurable visit abroad or after a business tour? Awkward. Should I joke or laugh to subtly make light of serious moments? Even that was silly. Tell him about two good friends who were no more? That would pain him. What then? Compliment him on how good he's looking? That would sound fake as I was told he had grown a beard, not having shaved in aeons, and dropped eight kilos in weight. My heart sank at the thought of encountering such an apparition of his former self. Frankly, I was at a loss for words on how to break the silence. Somewhere, I was a woman still in love and could have done anything in the book to get him into my world again! Order his favourite food, gatta and sanger with dal ki puri? That seemed more appropriate.

Struggling to get a foothold or even a toehold on the slippery slope of the quicksand of life, I wondered what his priorities would be when he had managed to get himself admitted in a Pune hospital, in the guise of a feigned illness, to take a breather from the morbid confines of prison. This was earlier, in September. Would he ask me to fly down to meet him during the time he was granted a reprieve in hospital?

When he was granted bail, would he first come to visit us at home or head straight to his own home?

~

I reckoned silently yet grievously that half my life was over but I had just about realized only a quarter of my dreams! Could I possibly reclaim the rest of my unrequited yearnings in the latter half? Or were the odds stacked against me?

Were the giant wheels of time on my side or were they spinning relentlessly against me?

My mobile rang just as these thoughts played out in my mind. I was inclined to ignore the call till I saw Mr Rajan, Surya's secretary's name, flash on my mobile. It must have been something important as the hearing was supposed to conclude by 5 p.m.

'Ma'am, I'm sorry to inform you that sir's bail has been refused for the third time.'

This sounded like a death knell as I gasped for breath. My heart raced furiously. I wanted to tear up the turquoise saree I had planned to wear on his return as the dreams that had kept me afloat were dashed to the ground once again.

'Cheer up, Aksh,' I said to myself. 'This is not your war. It's a world you left far behind. Do you need to revisit those insecurities and heartaches again?'

Alas, the voice of logic was drowned in the clamorous beats of the heart.

'Power is Poison...'

...AS SONIA GANDHI famously said. Power is perhaps the greatest opium of a megalomaniac mind, as also its downfall; except, like beauty, it too is ephemeral. And one who is visited by power is oblivious to what a transitory visitor it is in their life.

A part of me still belonged to Surya, my fragile heart in the grip of his destiny and the raging battles he was fighting. I was in the midst of this storm with heart and soul in abject surrender to its fury. There were no other choices. This was a battle to redeem his honour and salvage a human being's dignity, no matter what the odds.

Fearing for Surya's emotional and physical well-being in Yerawada Jail, I felt helpless in the face of his rogue political adversaries, who held a firm grip on the running of the prisons as well as the courts. During his first ten days in prison, I had heard that Yadav had issued orders to deliver Surya third-degree punishment. Indian prisons had been claimed by the National Human Rights Commission as having among the worst records of living conditions, illegal detentions and torture. The Maharashtra jail manual, which is part of the legal statute of the country, still vests authorities with the power to physically punish prisoners. A chilling account of the Malegaon blasts accused, Sadhvi Pragya, recorded in a video statement, sent shivers down my spine. Her lower body was paralysed due to the Maharashtra police 'beating her with leather belts at night, starving her for twenty-four days, verbally accusing her and making her watch pornographic recordings in the company of undertrials.'[*]

I chanced upon a report which stated the National Human Rights Commission had to take suo moto cognizance of predators in Indian jails. Convicts were tortured physically and mentally, good-looking young men in their early twenties being preferred targets of sodomy, by entire gangs that ruled the inmates. I read of a twenty-eight-year-old computer professional who had stopped shaving in order to look old, so as to avoid the preying eyes of those who would want to victimize him. Struck with the gloomiest of thoughts, I read on that there were organized gangs in Indian jails across the country, each one headed by a don: Haddi gang, Atte gang, Kikri gang, Biri gang… Allegiance to any one of them ensured access to mobile phones, cigarettes and protection from bullies of rival gangs. Often, when a young inmate was assaulted, the aggressors' friends watched in voyeuristic pleasure, multiplying the victim's humiliation. 'When a newcomer was masturbated upon to felicitate his arrival, the act was termed Colgate.'

From sodomy and rape the report turned to tales of freshers being beaten with steel plates as the victims ran about helplessly, while bystander inmates yelled and cheered, like watching a bullfight.

These sounded like gut-wrenching scenes of lives consigned to hell and damnation, the veracity of which was beyond doubt, in fact, under-reported!

Prisoners were sent to be reformed and punished, not

---

[*] *Source:* http://timesofindia.indiatimes.com/city/bhopal/Sadhvi-Pragya-narrates-police-torture-story-on-video/articleshow/45364870.cms

brutalized. This was barbaric in a civilized country. Could any of this be happening to Surya? Morbid and eerie reflections traumatized me endlessly.

Was this India, a liberal democracy? Or was it some barbaric, savage ISIS caliphate?

Just who was to blame for this heinousness when the Home Ministry was in the firm grip of the ruling party in the state, whom the police reported directly to? Inhuman behaviour of such savage propensity can only be attributable from the top down. Prison and judicial reforms were long overdue across India but were deferred to suit politicians, so as to retain a system that could intimidate political adversaries, if needed. Even Tamil Nadu's CM, Jayalalithaa, did not escape being ill-treated and holed up in a cell infested with mosquitoes and rats. That she was culpable in her disproportionate assets case was for the courts to decide. But who was responsible for her inhuman treatment if not her political opponents?

Industry, the voice of reason, the voice of the rich, famous and influential, was conveniently silent and apathetic on human rights, as this was far removed from their business-centric concerns. Sycophantic business czars lap-danced for their mega deals to the tunes of these venal politicians. Too much of their fiscal stakes were at odds if they spoke out in condemnation of injustices by the state, as for example, on the plight of undertrials. There was no crusader for the rights of the voiceless on several civic issues.

Arbitrariness ruled over democratic principles. The government was meant to function as the keeper of justice and perform its duty to protect the common man. Yet, the pendency of cases awaiting disposal was alarming in every court. Litigants suffered inordinate delays due to adjournments, a torture tactic used to the hilt by Surya's opponents to deliberately procrastinate his release.

↜

That night, I attended an intimate dinner of about forty-odd close friends. One of the guests was a big wheeler-dealer in arms, whom I had known over the years, highly polished in his mannerisms and with a great sense of humour. When one deals in nefarious businesses, somewhere at the back of your mind you are aware that it's a high-risk activity, where one is under constant media glare and scrutiny by the police, the enforcement directorate and the income tax authorities. These people are mentally prepared, knowing that they are perpetually under the scanner, to undergo a jailhouse rock for short spells, serve a part of the sentence if convicted, and pay their way out of it for the remaining tenure.

So did Peter Singh in his case. He got away with a short stint as he played for big stakes with those in power, winning them over instead of antagonizing the bigwigs.

'Akshraa, stop looking so crestfallen and erase that droopy look. The world hasn't come to an end with Suryaprakash in jail.'

'Peter, I am not exactly used to someone close to me going into confinement! It's not an everyday occurrence for me, you know!'

'Aksh! Cheer up,' Peter hugged me and said. 'During my stint in Tihar, I made some very good, lifelong pals. I lost weight as the food was so inedible and vegetarian. Don't you see how good I am looking now, silly girl? It was like a few months at a spa. With no air conditioning it felt like a natural sauna, a real detox for my otherwise toxic habits. No cell phones, so no business calls and chicks hounding me. It was peace, quiet and meditative thoughts...' The goofball almost thought of his quick in-and-out of jail stints as rehab, a joint the rich and famous visit by virtue of their vices; a knowing price they pay for their illicit wealth, to be sent in for forced penance to quit smoking, drinking and partying for a while. Small price for big money. What's the big deal?!

Peter went on to tell me how former telecom minister A. Raja and DMK MP Kanimozhi, accused and imprisoned in the 2G spectrum scam, had formed their own cricket teams to pass time in jail, spending time in the library, reading and teaching inmates subjects they were proficient in.

He regaled me with his foolish wisdom. His humour did distract me for sure.

∾

December 2015

Every phase of life brings with it a new morrow.

The day of Suryaprakash's release finally came on 14 December. He seemed anything but tired and downcast. The pep, the sizzle and the fizz, was in full swing. Our meeting was an animated, emotional connect, full of humour and warmth. Quite an anticlimax for both of us.

He had now re-entered the real world after nearly a year's absence. He needed to revive his mojo and his bruised psyche in order to rebuild his lost authority and regain the trust in leadership with employees, shareholders, financial institutions, bureaucrats and the government. He must have sensed the loss of his stature in the business world. It must have felt like staring at the pinnacle from ground zero, an arduous trek to the top ahead of him.

I anticipated the first encounter to be a monologue like with the sphinx that adorned the entrance to my home. I had imagined stony silences. When you're brought to your knees with nothing left in your hands, the only option was to say to God with a humble heart, 'Dear Lord, you got me this far. I now leave myself in your hands to take me where you will...'

The important thing was that Surya was out of the jaws of death, safely home again. The relief of seeing him securely out of prison and in the comfort of an air-conditioned home was huge. All else paled in contrast.

Being together, or being alone, was inconsequential. What took precedence was restoring normalcy in day to day living with a sound sense of emotional well-being.

~

Changed Lives

It was 7.25 p.m., five minutes before Surya was scheduled to arrive at my house, his ex-abode. I waited at the gate with my grandchildren, a thali in hand, laced with laddoos, rose petals and vermillion to greet him, while the auspicious Gayatri mantra played inside the house to be heard beaming right through the driveway up to the entrance. My heart sang with joy and I didn't care if the music was loud enough for the neighbours to hear. The first embrace as he alighted from the car was with Viraaj and Armaan, who held a rose each in their hands, their present for Surya which they had bought with their pocket money from the local florist. Only after that was a formal hug with me. I put a tilak on his forehead to welcome him, and raised my hands to offer the prasaad I had got from the temple I had visited in the morning as thanksgiving. Viru and Armaan eyed the laddoos, waiting for their turn to gobble them up. Oblivious to the reason of the festivity, they believed what they were told, that their doting 'Dadu' had just returned after a hectic business trip from London. They were more interested to open the presents Dadu had got them, from…hold your breath…Hamley's! They had asked for an airplane and dinky cars! Tiny hearts with tiny needs.

We went inside and only after Surya had finished dutifully indulging the kids, as they went to sleep by 8 p.m., did we get a chance to be alone. There was a palpable sense of security being cuddled by their grandfather and seeing the return of the eldest to the house. Children can't articulate but possess acute sensory perceptions, especially when it comes to survival and protection.

Then it was finally him and me. I wondered if I was meeting a broken man trying to reconnect to his past with despair and regret of the wasted months.

Though my own life was shattered years back, my dreams were still alive.

As for him, after this setback, I hadn't a clue what was his take at this stage of life. Would I see the old Surya with his natural flamboyance ever again? Conversation unfolded gradually as we uncorked the champagne. It was getting easier to unwind and connect. He had driven in his stretched limousine, suited in Armani, a strut in his gait, and jovial. Was this real? Was he camouflaging deep scars he would never allow me to peek into? I knew him too well for him to hide behind a fake laugh. He looked good, swanky and utterly at peace. Nowhere close to his age, younger than when he was done in. He didn't appear physically or mentally tired, nor overtly venomous towards his enemies. If revenge was a game plan, then it must be a silent, simmering anger that would play out with time, which I would never be privy to. Was this also real? No. He couldn't fake it this much: look good, talk well and with complete equanimity. Abnormal! A total contrast to the persona I thought I would encounter. It was getting better by the minute, considering how I had dreaded the first few moments of awkwardness.

I inquired why he had stayed a day longer in Pune after he was freed. He said he had witnessed the sorrow and helplessness of the poor undertrials who languished for years in jail and lacked paltry sums to even furnish a bail bond. 'Since I was privileged enough to have access to the best legal counsel in the country, I went back to say bye to my friends who had never had even ₹10,000 to defend themselves, and to assure them I would help as much as I could. I didn't want to leave without a meeting with them, and I also went back to thank some of the officers who were kind to me… Bachiyaa, you know, one day I even danced in jail. And I danced so well that they asked me to teach them too.' A sudden sadness overtook my expression. Mannequin-like, I froze.

There was a stabbing pathos in my perception of his story. Looking good, talking with humour and now dancing in jail and having inmates as friends! What more? Here was a man who had broken bread with heads of state and the highest echelons of international society, danced in the plushest of nightclubs and gorged on gourmet cuisine. It blew my mind. My respect and admiration for him as a human being was skyrocketing.

The heaviness was stifling, as I excused myself on a pretext of going to the loo. I bawled and wept like I hadn't since the day Mummy passed away some years back. Dancing in jail? Was this the dance of liberation after grief?

I reappeared a few minutes later, my kaajal smeared on the edge of my sari with which I had wiped my tears. He got up to embrace me. He said, 'These are your tears of joy, Akshraa. I am touched...' If only he knew the sadness beyond those tears of joy.

Fishing for sentiment, I asked, 'Did you miss your loved ones?'

He further stumped me, 'Of course. From time to time...' But he named no one, to my utter disappointment. I expected eulogies and lovelorn tributes as to how he had realized my worth in absentia; he said nothing of the sort.

Instead, he went on to say, 'I am a slave to nothing. The day I decided to quit smoking, I stubbed the butt and never looked back. You do know I can abstain from alcohol without ever missing it. I am not in acute discomfort without an air conditioner. Yes, the toilets were bad. I did my daily pranayaam and prayed twice a day, as I always do. I fasted for navraatraas, my biannual discipline, as you know. Now I have to conquer one last thing: my addiction for people I love. I have to become a little detached. Just a little...not that I am looking to completely relinquish worldly attachments. But this too I will overcome.' I gauged that he had gone past feeling like a victim but neither did he portray himself a victor; instead, he was just balanced and devoid of any trace of cynicism.

Had this joker been to a monastery or a prison?

~

I recall once accompanying Surya on a trip to Europe when he was on an acquisition spree to buy a sick textile unit. I was so proud of his achievement the day he signed the mega deal, I said, 'This evening calls for a celebration... One more company to add to your fleet of flagships. What a splendid moment, darling!' But he was unaffected by the new purchase, almost as though it was just another working day. In hindsight, I reflected as I remembered that he had shown a consistent equanimity through life's vicissitudes of elation and despair, joy and sorrow, wins and losses. It didn't strike me those days as those endearing traits escaped my sensitivities.

Cut to the present, nine years after this acquisition, Surya proceeded to explain his point of view briefly. 'Akshraa, let me get one fact straight. I acquired a lot of businesses two years before the fall of the Lehmann Brothers. You do understand, all businesses grow on leverage from banks and financial institutions, which is what I did. I had hoped to honourably repay the capital once these verticals turned profitable. Anything wrong in my premise or decision? Now, no oracle could have predicted this phenomenon was spiralling like a beast out of control. Once demand fell, my businesses were trapped in the downturn and I was left having to honour the companies' commitment to repay loans. If my collaterals were misused by a private lender, who behaved like a land-shark at the insistence of political heavyweights with vested interests, should I have succumbed to the arm-twisting? A civil case was converted to a criminal web of allegations against me. This was with an intent to usurp prime land at distressed prices far below market rates. I will fight this.

'If anything, my hardship has only strengthened my resolve. I am not weakened. And you should not be pained either. If one of the largest real-estate companies in India has had to sell off its non-core businesses to repay ₹20,000 crore to lenders, or one of the largest conglomerates is inundated with debts of over ₹100 lakh crore, surely my debts sound minuscule. Banks have mounting Non Performing Assets (NPAs) due to power, infrastructure, airlines and real-estate companies' inability to repay loans due to losses. If mega-corps are in distress, my businesses also suffered collateral damage due to the aftermath of the economic crisis. These are business cycles that play out which are beyond rational forecasts, you will agree? Lehmann was in 2008, we are in 2015. Seven years since, how gloomy has the economic scenario been? Who has been untouched by this crisis? Do you see a vibrant recovery anytime soon?' He continued, 'To that extent, yes, I am one of the victims of this slowdown, but a bigger victim of my destiny that I had to turn to land sharks who tried to exploit my business in distress.'

Surya's flow of contentions was completely logical. This was reminiscent of the Great Depression of the 1930s. Countries like Greece were still battling sovereign debt and nearing default, behemoths and millionaires in the US were still struggling to pull themselves out of the abyss they had dug themselves into. 'Who or what am I, but one lone individual affected by this financial tsunami?' he exclaimed.

This was a real-life example I had witnessed, so close to home, of the depressive impact of the global downturn.

∾

Punishment and imprisonment were meant to serve as a destination to purgatory and to self-cleanse in *Mein Kampf*, one's struggle of life. When law and justice confine an individual to a solitary hell, it has a purpose of chastising. It also can work in reverse. An inmate's mind is so muddied, mired and sullied in hatred that it could deteriorate to revenge, and get further entrapped in negative cyclicals of karmic actions and reactions. Either of the two phenomenon could have played out in Surya's psyche too.

This day was to be my moment of true learning. This was rare stoicism on display. Something to imbibe.

My reflections thereafter were that if there is one harsh

reality in India, it is this: 'we castigate failure across the board.' Be it with our cricketing captains who failed a test, an ex-PM who had the highest integrity, or PM Modi who was perceived as a scaled-down image of his former self after the debacle of the Delhi elections or, for that matter, a film star who failed in an anticipated blockbuster. Let's know that like humans are mortals who can fall, businesses also suffer the same fate. No business is 'Too Big to Fail'. The emotional stigma we attached to failure was huge when one was down and out. But despite Surya's diminishing fortune, nothing detracted from past laurels. He was just a bad judge of character and too trusting of courtiers, relying on sycophants who presented him with embellished business plans that he failed to see through.

A Sincere Attempt to Bridge Chasms...

December 2015

Two weeks after Suryaprakash's release, once he found his bearings, we flew to the Maldives on a vacation. When he suggested the holiday, I blushed to even think of a night together. Tiny tendrils of love were gradually emerging.

As a few grey streaks had begun to appear in my hair, I was coming to terms with ageing, loving the silvery grey tones to life. In youth, perceptions are clear, with bold delineations of seeing life in definitive colours of black or white. Grey, to my mind, was finding the beauty between binaries. Every situation was not black or white; right or wrong; love or war.

Everything didn't have to be interpreted in extremes. There were middle paths, where secrets of peace and solutions resided, with perhaps more intelligent, intuitive ways to bridge the unbridgeable.

We went to the island resort with minds wide open to possibilities. Possibilities of a final ending or everlasting love.

Being together in the Maldives was the swansong of a thousand unfulfilled desires, a thousand unanswered questions and a thousand dreams strewn like dry autumn leaves scattered in the sands of time. You could feel them between silences. Those feelings of unrequited love and unresolved grief alternated with moments of reviving affection that could set the night aflame with passion, like a candle burning brightest before its end. Nay! A red amber light in the dusk of one's life, the last flicker of love. Except that it would be a love devoid of the zealous ownership that comes with commitment, this time around. By now, did I really crave the permanence that comes with ownership?

I had walked with rubble under my feet till they bled, to arrive at the pinnacle that I now stood on. I frequently lost my way in a maze of labyrinthine corridors of painful memories that greeted me like phantoms through those travails. By now, I had experienced a power born of knowledge that would never let me look back at the helplessness of yesteryears.

The presidential suite upon the lagoon at the Taj in Maldives was bedecked with flowers, the fragrance of roses wafting through the room, their aroma overpowering one's olfactory senses. It was the most breathtaking sight to see the suite festooned for my arrival with the care Suryaprakash took in his instructions to the hotel staff.

We talked a lot in those few days.

'Surya, like any girl in her youth, I too had a dream. I had hoped it was an unending reverie till the end of time. As life unfolded with us, pain was no more pain, because time had numbed the wounds, though they never really healed. I waited years for that coveted moment of sincere, heartfelt remorse from you; if only you could have expressed just a tinge of regret and reached out with a warm embrace to say you cared enough to never let go of me, even if you didn't mean it… For the love we shared, it's a lie I would have believed. Till I learnt to make peace with a dream that was never to be. Years back, you bartered me as a sacrificial lamb for your selfish ways. Today, between my rights and your wrongs stands a wall, a silent, angry space between us. It is a life I have chosen to never look backwards upon. I prefer to be alone. Or semi-alone! We come alone and leave alone, don't we?

'Togetherness in a lifetime is just an illusion. Aren't we all alone anyway? Akshu, let's look ahead, shall we?'

'I treasure with deep affection, Surya, every small and large gesture to win my heart. It somewhat mitigates the pain of the past. You and I are evolved people. Only bigots take rigid stands. Sadly, we grew miles apart instead of a supportive love that should have seen two humans grow together as one.'

'You only feud with people you belong to, a stranger has no domain in your heart,' he said to me.

'I have freed myself of the fear that used to immobilize and grip me,' I said. 'The fear that you would one day walk away from me. If today I am trying to meet you midway, I do so from a position of strength, not necessity. I have grown from within. If I maybe want you back in my life, it is for love and not out of servility...I always awarded you the pride of place in the innermost shrine of my heart but today I have moved miles away from an inequitable and feudal marriage. I can dispense with it gladly! We are equals or nothing.'

'I did think adversities bring people closer, for what you and I shared in pain, in laughter and in joy was far more enormous than the divisive forces that tore us apart. I have taken a moment to pause and rest, only to look back at the pleasurable distance we travelled together. Hopefully, if we can rise above trivia, Akshraa, maybe we can walk hand in hand with a firmer grip and deeper love till the end of time?' he responded.

'Forever!' I spurned that thought with my residual cynicism.

What in life is forever? 'Surya, there were many misgivings between both of us in the years we were together. As some years have lapsed, possibly a side to you, as also with me, must have gotten to love, or learnt to love that independence.'

'But I think we still care enough, Akshraa,' he said, 'to give it a fair try to work things out, if you are open to a reconciliation. I really and truly thought a lot about you and us during those months in confinement. I can't force you to change your stance. I can't make you love me. But I can pledge the rest of my years to make up for all that I must have done to hurt you. I want you for the rest of my life. I will take those sanctimonious vows again and promise not to ever cause you a moment's grief ever again. I want to rebuild my empire and rebuild a beautiful life with you from scratch. I cannot do it alone. I need you. Please allow me to feel that today is the first day of the rest of our life? Can I feel, with your loving support, that my life has just begun?'

Tears poured down in a cascade of grief. I had no instant answers. 'Surya, honestly, after you walked away, I felt devoid of any vestiges of self-esteem. I had offered the best of me and the finest years of my productive life at the altar of a sacred bond with you. I laid my poverty bare, prostrating myself before you in oblation, just so you would give me a small niche in your heart. What was I to do when you abandoned me, leaving me in that state of shock? Forgive? Recriminate? Get into a war zone fighting for property rights? What was I to tell society? The children? Turn to a doctor, lawyer or shrink?'

∾

On one of the evenings, we had dinner on an isolated reef that protruded on the waters from the atoll formation, where only four people could be seated. It was like a private dining area surrounded by water, suspended in the infinity of turquoise aqua as far as the eye could see. The sparkling white sandy beaches, crystal clear lagoons, colourful corals and warm seas with undisturbed marine life made one feel in sync with nature. The four corners had been illuminated with mashaals, the gush of sea breeze erratically tossing the flames emanating from the poles around.

Earth, wind, fire and water, in a mystical confluence of elements, converged on this magical setting, as two chefs indulged us with fine-dining rarities, while a trio came by to serenade us. Even if two people hated each other, the lure of romancing within this ambience was irresistible. But honestly? I still loved him. Though the passion had whittled over the years, a teeny-weeny corner of my heart was more than open to reconcile, or I wouldn't have been here with him.

It was tough to say which emotions could get stirred as we interacted. When love wanes, whatever the remnants, it's a long trek to intimacy and normalcy. Years back when we split, nothing had prepared me for the break-up and how to live with the absence of the man I was used to seeing by my bedside each morning. Today, there were contrarian pulls emotionally, as Surya reached out with a renewed affection, 'Bachiyaa, let's hold hands through the day and promise this is no time for goodbyes anymore. I want and need you…all of you, as long as I live… all of you, for the rest of my life. This life, the next life-after-life… ad infinitum….' I wanted the same, though was too proud to say it out loud.

We took a break as I strolled around the hotel area by myself for an hour. I found those defining, life-altering and transformative moments only occurred between pauses, between spaces, from the ramparts of one's inner silence. Whilst in action mode, it is only reactionary reflexes that play out; it is in the stillness that I effaced my truth, blotting out a symphony of sorrows and an avalanche of memories of some parts of our past that kept resurfacing periodically. Dystopia lies not outside of us, I reckoned, but is deeply embedded within, and that required a silent resolution.

I reasoned that love reignited in middle age could be far more symbiotic and fulfilling as the second time around, we were both open to exploring a life together, suffused with forgiveness, penitence and serendipity, by trying not to invoke a past that could have been the epitaph of love. I didn't want to rule out a reconciliation.

Infatuation was when you perceived somebody as absolutely perfect, but love was realizing fallibility and shedding that idealism, yet celebrating synergies and those crazy idiosyncrasies that define each one of us. Were we humorous and humanistic enough towards each other to allow that interplay of independence, so different from the dependency and control dramas of the past?

Though something had died within both of us, we were holding on to what remained by a fragile string. I decided not to force things but to just allow them to happen. Our pulls towards each other seemed a 'demon one could neither resist nor understand'.

~

We resumed our emotional negotiations from where we had left off. 'Surya, you must know that my years of aloneness were moments of reckoning, as much as resolution. If it was the will of God that I was meant to be alone forever more, so be it. Looking around me, I searched for icons who transcended a life beyond marriage by exploring the lives of leaders who were ignited by a zeal larger than themselves, people who changed the course of history. Whether through death, desertion or choice, those icons remained single because they were fired by a mission that was larger than personal vaccuum. Indira Gandhi, Suu Kyi, Atal Bihari Vajpayee, Narendra Modi, Princess Diana, Hillary Clinton…became exemplary sources to draw strength from. Inspirational as a parable, their growth path taught me to think beyond a life of love. If there's love, great! If there wasn't, I wasn't going to put my life on hold. In my case, I was not a national figure but I could try to elevate my level of thought and occupation to go beyond my selfish moorings.'

'Akshu, I have no desire to leave you alone ever again. It's good that you've become a loner and survived the grief I must have given you. One day, I too am answerable to God above. Allow me to penetrate these formidable walls you have built around yourself. I will never forsake you for anything in the world. You can scream, shout, cry and get it out of your system. But I will never stop loving you with renewed fervour. You have to give us another chance…' he implored.

'I am not done with what I have to say as yet!' I felt my tone change, despite his softness. 'Surya, now that we are face to face, I would like to share a harsh truth with you. I want to tell you the darkest secret I have withheld from you. Years back when you hurt me, I had begun to hate you and that festered for a long time. But I never had the guts to walk out on you though those gnashes stabbed me each day. Stabbed by the only one in life I ever depended upon, because I lacked the money to sustain the lifestyle you had got me addicted to. I suffered the pain of your betrayals silently, never wanting to even share the same room with you. Today, I come close to being canonized in my own eyes because I still care unconditionally in my own way…

when I least need you for sustenance. I can afford to love you without your money because God showered me with so much of my own, plus the wealth I created on my own when I worked for HCL. But compared to the lifestyle you indulged me in, my means were inadequate twenty years down the line. It's only after Mom and Dad that I came into a huge inheritance.

'Maybe what I feel for you now isn't love. Perhaps it's higher than love. It's devotion and gratitude, being beholden for the life you exposed me to. You showed me a world which I never knew existed. But it also felt like the sadistic fattening of a prey before its kill, because you abandoned me thereafter.

'I didn't beg for that world you opened up for me. I could have done with much, much less. And believe me, after we split, I was so much more at peace with a little less luxury. I begged for your love and respect more than anything else. You were my only emotional support after my parents passed away. That's the truth.'

The relief of unburdening myself by admitting to the scheming side of me dropped the burden of guilt like the weight of an albatross round my neck. I felt lighter and better. When one is hurt, there is a wily side inherent in every human being that acts as a self-protective shield. I dropped that shield with my admissions. It really and truly didn't matter if it was going to prejudice Surya's mind. I had little to lose.

On the contrary, what he did then was to embrace me warmly. Perhaps my candour struck him. We were done playing mind games. His voice choked and I saw tears well up within his eyes, 'Akshraa, you win. As they say, "the winner takes it all, the loser standing small". I can only ask for another chance to hold on to you. I will bend. But I've been through too much myself to ever break, should you reject my apologies. The last call is yours.'

I didn't feel like he was going to yield or implore much

more than this. He was too proud. I sensed this was where his masculine pride was drawing the line between wanting me or just letting go from here on. He had expressed his remorse. He had reached out in gestures. But that was it!

Tense moments…

The ball was back in my court.

I now felt slightly insecure, feeling sucked into the vortex of a whirlwind of emotions.

↝

It was past midnight as we sat sipping Bailey's Irish Cream after dinner. Sitting on that isolated reef surrounded by emerald green aqua, we were two souls lost in time, space and eternity. Nothing, and no one, mattered then, like a moment in infinity. I felt the breeze play with my hair, the white sand tingle my toes, my saree swaying waywardly with the wind, as we kissed, held hands and got up to stroll back to our rooms. Except, I wondered if we would spend the night in the same room or in adjacent rooms, like we had done on the previous two nights.

Love Defined but One Part of the Woman that Is Me

Having mulled over our conversations, I expressed an unconventional route to an emotional impasse. 'Surya, should you agree, can we decide to live together as man and wife but in a non-traditional way? Whilst our hearts and spirits remain in unison, we will never share a physical space together? A status I choose to define as "the single married woman". I live life at multiple levels and have developed diverse interests. Those have come to define my "astitva", my regained pride in myself. From centring my world around a single relationship, I have worked hard to get out of being obsessive about any one aspect of life. I do care enough not to let go of you in this lifetime. Can we agree to singlehood within marriage?'

In the end, I too craved the universal urges of womanhood for intimacy, companionship and self-perpetuation through a man–woman bond. Except this time around, I had learned the utter futility of surrendering myself to allow anyone to sublimate or lord over my life. The difference was that in my youth, being committed to marriage was my everything. Today, it was but a small part of a whole. In my younger years, the death of love spelt the end of my world. But as I grew older, I enjoyed the torrid flow of the river of life that could never be impeded. It had to move on. Life was energy in motion, as I never allowed myself to remain in a space of status quo.

I found that only three kinds of people dwelled in a state of remaining fixated: people who were risk-averse, manic depressives or thought bigots. Luckily, I escaped all these states of being.

Was it then that the world was my playground, as the French termed it, *On joue sur la terre*? My stage of unfettered liberation? Liberation meant it was time for mirth, love, laughter and lightness to enter this heavy drama that had been playing out for years. Isn't lightness man's normal state of being ultimately?

I was old enough to affirm that no one completes you like you yourself. Half a circle is but a crescent. But the lustre and luminescence of the half-moon was also very beautiful!

A crescent I would remain, retaining its incandescent splendour as a single married woman. And in the end, thick in the whirlwinds of my thoughts...that was my final call.

On that isolated reef, where we sat over dinner on the last evening of our holiday, I wondered if life was throwing something beautiful back at me. Was I so blinded by past prejudices that I was not noticing love coming back to me? Was life giving me a message I was not receptive to? Where the elements of earth, wind, fire and water confluence, could I not see the 'sangam' of a sacred marriage coming together? Two mighty streams, though flowing at their own pace, do ultimately conjoin, don't they? I was also ultimately powerless to resist the force of this torrent.

Nothing is forever. Forever was a myth. I craved to reclaim a lost life, lost moments, lost laughter, and lose the tears I wept. There was no afterlife. That was a lie too. This moment was my time to live out every fantasy and savour the seven deadliest sins. I chose to live the best of both worlds, of being single and loving my freedom, yet married and loving the togetherness of a new state of being.

A single married woman.

An identity within an identity, yet amorphous and blithe, free as the wind.

This, then, was that rare moment of convergence, when life seemed to come together in synchronicity.

Alone I would remain.

But wedded to the one and only love of my life, Surya.

Today, as I look back from atop the pinnacle of time and wisdom, our years apart seemed just a pause in the infinitude of a lifetime. I lied to myself and the world that I didn't care but Surya was my world.

My tears.

My joys.

My laughter.

My life's every heartbeat.

He owned me.

And I belonged to him.

I didn't choose him.

My heart did.

Twice over.

Postscript

'Art is the cry of the mind exhausted by its own rebellion.'
—Albert Camus

To my esteemed reader,

I so concurred with the French philosopher and activist Camus when I wrote this novel, as the message and leitmotif that compelled my script lay painfully dormant within me for years. However, shaping the protagonist's character and the events that unfolded came entirely from my emotional memory. In the novel, I live vicariously through Akshraa, as she embodies my yearning to rewrite the rules of femininity: owning up to your ambition is brave, beautiful and sexy!

I request you, the reader, to treat the story as a parable, a work of fiction or a near reality of the protagonist Akshraa's existentialist crisis. Through her triumph over adversities, hers is the suppressed voice of a lot of Indian women craving expression, uncomfortable to own up to ambition. I found that serving a parable through the oeuvre of a love story would be easier to relate to in order to open closed minds, as love is a universal language that binds. I use the challenges Akshraa faces to explore issues that concerned me deeply: the fault lines of male supremacy in denying freedom of creativity and expression to women. So when Akshraa is young and a working professional I exemplify the middle-age void that strikes any woman who has not sustained her interests, placing family selflessly at the altar, at the cost of her self-evolution. When one nurtures a pastime and passion of one's calling, it's also a form of prayer, a creative quietude, that enhances self-worth. My convictions on these thoughts led me to pen a script with a strong social conscience.

Years of a woman's life pass by in her prime, catering to the needs of family and children, depriving herself of pursuing her vocation. Then what stares her in the face at middle age is a very lonely life, where no one can feel her pain nor un-cry her tears of a lifetime gone by, where she ignored her own progress, whether it's a hobby or following a career path. I chose to come out of my purdah and drop the veil, by shattering the silence within that leapt into my pages. I would have felt emotionally and intellectually disloyal to my convictions if the author in me did not impersonate Akshraa's angst, though it took me down a painful path of excavating some of my deepest memories from within to cast them onto Akshraa's character.

The Indian woman is a beautiful bouquet comprising myriad hues of courage, yet she remains a fragile and vulnerable damsel-in-distress. She is a paradox of duty and playfulness; virtuous, yet charmingly seductive in her femininity. Her ambition is her badge of honour to flaunt, for having a brain is sexier than sex.

Celebrate your identity and individualism through any medium that you find is your forte: through the lucrative world of commerce or the creative world of arts. Marriage is a great synergy amongst two souls to bring out the best in each other without stunting one for the other.

India is changing in its attitude towards women very gradually. The restiveness on television debates rages across media on the topic of gender equality, an issue which is no longer relegated to 'soft' lifestyle articles in glossies or consigned to the back pages of newspapers. Ultimately, the strife of the Indian woman integrates with the global movement of empowerment, where financial self-sufficiency is the only route to gender parity.

I stumbled upon the former director of The Institute of Economic Growth, economist Bina Aggarwal's findings, which I paraphrase, as also quote lavishly from, long after I had completed my manuscript, and which I found so corroborative to my own work and convictions. Bina is accredited with getting the Hindu Succession Amendment Act of 2005 passed, due to which most Indian women enjoy the same rights of inheritance as men. Yet, even today, few own immovable property or agricultural land titles in their name.

'Ownership of an asset enhances not only a woman's status, decision-making and bargaining power within the family and community, but protects her from domestic violence.' Bina's findings were derived from a study, albeit of a small sample-size in Kerala, that led to her findings that 'while 49 per cent of property-less women faced beatings from spouses, the figures diminished to 18, 10 or even 7 per cent respectively, for women who owned land or a home', deterring domestic violence, substantiating my hypothesis in powering this narrative.**

I don't believe in binary definitions in the identity of womanhood as either just a homemaker or a working professional. She is all of that, and much more... Neither should she be a

---

**Bina Aggarwal, 'Indian Women Must Chart Their Own Path', interview with Kaveri Bamzai, *India Today Woman*, February 2016.

helpless and passive bystander to her trysts. Au contraire, today, she is becoming argumentative and questioning of her rights, making her the epic Daughter of India. The onus lies upon her to seize opportunities to embark on a virtuous cycle of 'earn-spend-save-and-empower' herself in a meaningful way that endorses her self-worth, one which will ultimately support her spouse's efforts, as also make her an asset to his life.

To my incredulity, I found it a sad reflection to read that rising literacy levels amongst women in urban India, despite the job opportunities which globalization had opened up, did not adequately increase the percentage of working women in cities. According to the findings of a study by eminent economists Surjit Bhalla and Ravinder Kaur, the rate of engagement of women in the labour pool was 'not very dissimilar from that prevailing in most Islamic countries.'[***]

Conversely, due to dire poverty and need, statistics of working rural Indian women from poor and low levels of family income remained higher than in cities, just in order to supplement family wages to earn two square meals a day. Neither were the benefits of education a guarantee of self-reliance or economic independence even for women in the uppermost strata, as the end destination of literacy was finding an eligible groom amongst status-seeking families. These were cultural and familial prejudices that wives found hard to liberate themselves from, as few women who married into affluent homes felt the need to shrug off constricting societal norms. If anything, it remained a status-halo in not pursuing a career amongst the affluent. In percentage terms, the number of financially empowered women in India is miniscule.

[***]Barkha Dutt, *The Unquiet Land*, Aleph Book Company 2016.

My take is not a purely feminist reaction, though empathetic to the suffering of women. As a vote bank, she is bigger than any caste or community in India, comprising 48 per cent of the population. There's an ailing side to society that has prevailed for centuries. Laws and attitudes are not gender equal. The indoctrination from childhood is subjugation to a husband or father. Nothing wrong in having gratitude for the male provider, your father who brought you up, or your husband who is the breadwinner. But what happens to a girl who grows into womanhood? She's in quest of cerebral fulfilment, a bud waiting to blossom and bloom. Who is stifling her spirit? Society? Or the constraints she puts on herself? Even at best, if she's educated and an earning member, most women still lack financial knowledge or skills in investing, which is ever so vital to learn in order to secure themselves for the future.

Life can be hurtful, extremely painful. But it is never the end of the world. If the only identity one has had is one that stems from dependency on love and marriage, it's a life half-lived. In a hybrid of a fictional 'self-help' genre, my mission is to see womanhood break away from the shackles of dependency. PM Modi said, 'We cannot achieve success if 50 per cent of our population, which is women, are locked at home.'

Contemporary love speaks a cosmic language of equity, self-respect and co-creation of life. It does not place man at the helm and woman as a slave, dependent on emotional or financial crumbs, or largesse for which she ought to be beholden eternally into abject surrender, and consequently enmeshed in a situational deadlock till the courts give her a reprieve, should a marriage go bad.

Her time to start living her dreams and on her terms is Anytime! Now? This instant! Eulogizing unrequited love makes for great, forlorn poetic verse. But day-to-day life is not poetry, nor an escape from harsh truisms which have to be dealt with grace.

The challenges Akshraa faces are pretty much the inevitable travails failed relationships leave behind: alienation, redeeming self-esteem, single parenting, mothering, divorce, survival and livelihood…multiple demons I've unleashed in the diary.

The stronger message is that Truth triumphs when you live in adherence to your tallest beliefs, yielding when you must, but never bending your head before 'insolent might'. Go it alone if you must, because the road is lonely. But, when one possesses a strong moral compass, one is able to explore and optimize a God-given potential fearlessly in order to withstand any reverses.

After having read through the book, you will be convinced that the route to salvation is through self-sufficiency that comes through financial wisdom. In or out of a relationship, when you are armed with that knowledge, you need not depend on anybody in this world for security, love, respect or honour. It depends on you. It's in your hands to redeem your astitva, and develop the gifts you were born with. That discovery of Self is the greatest motivator, and one that completes a person, making a spouse an emotional and financial asset to the significant other.

If I have achieved the task of conveying this message, I consider my work as 'love's labour' won, which I bequeath to you, my friend and reader.

Stay empowered,
Bindu Dalmia

Acknowledgements

Writing a book is a lonely arduous trek into the wilderness of thought experiments. One necessarily needs guinea pigs to test ideations and incubate ideas. In that process, some family members and friends became the book's muses, as I drew from their strengths to compile a composite whole. In equal measure, I am obliged to the critics who nailed the flaws with objective foresight. They were my guides.

I want to thank my muses and guides, each of whom helped shape my thoughts. These were the dramatis personae that played a part on the stage of my life.

Foremost, I dedicate this book to my departed parents, who thought they had left me in good hands and well-settled in life. I am, in a way, thankful that those were the abiding memories that must have stayed in their hearts when they left for their heavenly abode. If they are watching me from above today, they would be smiling at the journey I've traversed since, where I can look back with pride that I never allowed destiny or man to break me. With their perennial blessings I know nothing can impede my evolutionary journey onwards.

To my Guru, Yogi Ashwini, for grounding me in my astitva by teaching me a few harsh truths of life. When one is infatuated and seduced with the play of maya and the alternations of 'dhoop-chaun', it's hard to believe all of life is but an illusion and the only abiding karma is service to the underprivileged: man or animal. As mortals, in our youth we question this but yield to it by mid-age. Being a near-atheist, I was not a pliant 'shishu' but an inquisitive and errant student who had multiple questions to ask of Yogi ji, especially on my disbelief in the fatalistic laws of past-life karma as an explanation of present-life strife.

To my son Nikhil, my kid brother, my joy, my sunshine, my 'upper'... for his endless humour and optimism, for holding my fragile hand when I was at my lowest. If we as elders don't learn from our children, we would remain retarded adults missing out on an exciting New World order.

To my daughter-in-law Payal, for prodding me to script the story, her childish inquisitiveness apart!

To my grandchildren, Vansh Raj and Aditya Veer, my Luv and Kush, my amaanat... Each morning when you come into Daadi's room, I know the sound of your footsteps from a distance. Like sacred chants...ringing of some temple bells from afar, as the tiny feet come closer, those sounds turn into my prayer, my only reason for being.

To Anjali Burman, my childhood friend and mentor, who held my hand like an angel through every step of my life, especially my 'lost years'.

To my sister Asha Sharma, for the contagious feistiness that she inherited from my mother, which unfortunately bypassed my DNA! A modern-day version of eternal youth, like the glamorous legend Joan Collins, she kept kindling the fire in me to reignite each time the candle flickered.

To my soul sisters, Neeru Puri and Rano Singh. Every holiday with them was like a spiritual 'off-site', where I recreated myself each time we travelled together, catching yellow butterflies that inspired me to write more often after I re-energized myself.

To my brother-in-law, Shiv Nadar, who gave me wings when I was unfolding from the chrysalis of self-doubt in my most formative years.

To my dear friend Ravi Dhariwal, CEO of Bennett-Coleman, who conferred upon me a rare honour by inviting me on the august panel of writers for *Economic Times* blogs.

To my gym friends at Amatra, who never let the smile fade from my face or let me step away from the treadmill of life. My true muses, they taught me how to think young, or I could have been doomed to dwelling on middle-age hypochondria, like cholesterol or arthritis.

To Kanishka Gupta and the editorial team at Rupa Publications, for editing and downsizing my script, weeding the grain from the chaff, thankfully.

To Kapish Mehra, ever so energized as the young are! Thank you for showing spontaneity the day you received my first mail. I believed I had a story to tell.

And finally, you, the reader, for honouring me with the indulgence of holding this book in your hands.

Praise for the book

Salim Khan, veteran screenwriter, one half of the prolific writing duo, Salim-Javed:

I have known Bindu for years, but unaware of her latent skills as a wordsmith. When she discussed the idea of her storyline and fiction-with-a-conscience with me a year back, I liked it very much, as it was about the travails of most women craving to carve a distinct identity for themselves by pursuing a passion, within a happy marriage, or otherwise in order to possess a higher self-worth. To my surprise, she metamorphosed it into an interesting book very soon. I have liked the way she has brought out the dark side of the upper strata of Indian society. One would have understood if the same was written by a 'have not', but the fact that she has written this from the vantage of an incisive insider's portrayal of having lived a privileged life, depicts that she has, what I would term, 'divine dissatisfaction'. When the soul is in sufferance, it craves an outlet to create, striving to reach out to God or man through the medium of art. I know through experience that all art is born of pain…

I quoted to Bindu a verse I had deeply felt myself:

Aasoon nikal aiyyein,
tho khud poonchieyga,
Log poonchenge,
tho saudaa karenge.

She sat in stunned silence, imbibing this harsh truth of life. So she asked me with a sense of resigned pessimism, as someone older and wiser, 'Salim saab, does that make us all hapless victims, katputhlis to our fate?'

The Diary of a Lutyens' Princess is a must-read for all those who aspire to get married, for those who were married and have gone their ways, as equally for those who are married and are trying hard to make it work.

There are a few people who understand Bindu, but '*Bindu ko samajhna mushkil hi nahin, namumkin hai*'.

❧

Salman Khan, top Bollywood actor, reigning at the top of the charts for a decade:

The book brought tears to my eyes. I loved Akshraa as a woman who endured her travails with fierce pride and a strong resolve, who sacrificed for love, yet never compromised on values. Poignant, sensitive and inspirational, Akshraa is the soul of the Indian woman, repressed by male dominance, yearning to flower.

❧

Shiv Nadar, founder and chairman of HCL and the Shiv Nadar Foundation:

From my mind, heart, memory and as I write…

Bindu had been an enigma since the day I met her, a charming young college student from LSR, just about to be married. I preferred the name Gayatri, though. She was thereafter on her way to Calcutta, setting up home there, and had a lovely child in September 1975…

A few years had gone by, but we met from time to time on family occasions, as she used to frequent Delhi often. Clearly, I found something was missing… Something to keep her achievement and motivation upped. I have personally done TAT Analysis, and could do to one in a conversation. I found that she was A+ in Achievement and Motivation, and would be a straight-A winner. So, I invited her to join HCL at a managerial position. We aggregated Coal, Energy, Railways and institutional sales and marketing, and formed a group, OSCAR, which she headed at a young age. This was a structural paradigm deployed by IBM in those years, way back in the 1980s, when they were a transnational, with some of their prototypes in business worth emulating, before they left India, just as HCL was scaling up.

She was looked up to by her executives without exception. She led them like a classic general: was in front and in the trenches with them. Win they did, defying industry benchmarks of that time, in surpassing performance yardsticks of peers. I had set the bar high, very tall indeed, in quantifying deliverables. Without exception, most of her colleagues and members of her team in later years branched out to excel in other companies in India and overseas, heading behemoths today.

But the genesis of that core team was embedded within this cell, where Bindu's residence was a regular stopover as the port-of-call, the hang-out after office hours to strategize… There was a fire in them, so motivated was her guerrilla marketing team. She often generously attributed its success to the 'Shiv Nadar factory of mind-machines in thought-leadership', as she once said to me, when failure was not an option, and achieving goals an imperative. They dreamt big and with a passion in those years when the industry was nascent.

I concur with what she writes about this genre of professionals, who worked under a module of what I construed as 'intrapreneurs'. Put simply, this was an experiment in engaging professionals to their optimum, where they worked and felt like sheltered entrepreneurs, albeit within a large organization. But the risk, rewards, and profits mimicked ownership. Virtual ownership. So the incentive to remain 'paranoid' kept the team on hi-octane, only to surprise with their results and performance, year on year.

Her recap on the chapter on HCL is a beautiful recall of an era gone by, full of fond memories for me too…

She writes with her heart, as she worked with her heart.

~

Dimple Kapadia, iconic Bollywood actress:

The book truly encapsulates what it means to be a woman of today.

Akshraa's story of her struggles and triumphs won by an indomitable spirit will be an inspiration to every woman out there who wants to live her life on her own terms.

~

Sudhir Mishra, award-winning film director and screenwriter, recipient of three National Awards as well as Chevalier de L'Ordre des Arts et des Lettres conferred by the French government:

The book is a scathing portrayal of Lutyens' Delhi, an oasis of private splendour amidst an ocean of deprived humanity. Akshraa, the protagonist, is a beautiful bouquet of womanhood comprising myriad hues. A damsel in distress, she is courageous, yet fragile; a paradox of duty and playfulness, as she rewrites the rules of femininity.

~

Kapil Dev, former cricketer and captain of the Indian cricket team:

I first met Bindu in Kolkata as a young debutante, just beginning my career in cricket. Over my association with her since nearly thirty years, I never imagined or realized she possessed such a flair for writing.

~

Mira Kulkarni, Founder and MD, Forest Essentials, rated amongst the twenty most powerful women in business by *Fortune* India:

With razor-sharp wit and intellect, [Bindu] narrates the story of Akshraa's tumultuous life…makes for very insightful and interesting reading.

A perfectly manicured hand turns the deep rich velvet surface, to see another level below, not quite so beautiful, not quite so perfect.

A beautifully written satire spanning five decades, the central theme devolving on the evolution of a young girl with dreams in her eyes, to a woman of substance, in control of her script in life.

~

Indira Jaisingh, former Additional Solicitor General of India, Padma Shri awardee and member of the UN Committee for the Elimination of Discrimination Against Women:

While I have represented the rich and the famous, as equally women who are economically deprived, I have always been struck by the fact that the common denominator of most problems within a marriage are similar, which is denial of their economic rights within marriage. There is only one common civil code in operation: the 'common code of inequality'.

The Indian woman is asserting her constitutional and personal rights more fiercely than ever before, as India is changing, though very gradually. My cause célèbre remains to continue to support the weaker and less empowered women, and fight the fault-lines of male supremacy.

~

Yogi Ashwini, Dhayan Foundation:

In a paean to womanhood, Bindu in her unique way extols the 'Devi', the divine Shakti dormant in every woman who possess the attributes of Mahavidya and Mahamedha, supreme knowledge and supreme intellect. She is the primordial source of all creation who sustains the universe and one who dwells within every woman.

~

Minu Bakshi, famous author, linguist and poet, conferred the prestigious 'Order de Isabella la Catolica', the second-highest award given to any foreigner for her outstanding services to Spain and Spanish Language, by the Government of Spain:

When I asked Bindu to translate some of my poetry from Urdu, she found in my verse the voice of love that she had always wanted to make her own. It was as if she had found the thread to weave her own dreams entwined with mine, as she made my poetry far more beautiful than I had originally written. I treasure those translations which, truth be told, are both hers and mine.

For the die-hard romantic that Bindu is, I pen these lines for her *Diary*:

Ye ada hai tumhare jeene ki,
Chot khaate hue bhi, muskurate ho tum...

Zinda wo tere paane ka armaan ab bhi hai,
Dil mein humaare dard ka toofan ab bhi hai...

~

Kishore Bhimani, veteran sports journalist:

The reading is extremely entertaining. Calcutta 1967 was our era. The Naxalites on one side, the raucous Park Street joints and the club-life on the other made for a stark contrast, and I enjoyed reliving it. Yes, it has often been said that life is all about contrasts and paradoxes and Bindu has chronicled it amazingly.

~

Vikram Khanna, ex-economist at the IMF, Washington D.C.:

From the extracts I have read, I detect two narratives. One is an insider's view from a perceptive observer of the world of India's uber-rich at a time of economic transformation. It is a bubble world of fluid and brittle relationships, high ambition and achievement, but also decadence and a disconnection with the grim realities of India. Bindu has captured this well. The second narrative is that of a young girl breaking the shackles of her suffocatingly conservative upbringing and losing her innocence as she gets caught up in the high life. There would surely be many stories of this in the New

India. But Bindu tells it with wit and fearless candour.

❧

C.P. Gurnani, CEO, Tech Mahindra, chosen as the Ernst and Young Entrepreneur of the Year, CNBC Asia's India Business Leader of the Year, as also the Business Standard CEO of the Year:

Bindu you are a rock star...a role model of independent thinking and having the freedom of choice...to influencing many a lives like mine. The book represents Bindu in many senses, it's new-age and yet a reflection of core grounded values, bold and yet makes you think.

❧

Mahabanoo Mody-Kotwal, theatre personality and the producer of *Vagina Monologues* in India, chosen as one of the 50 most powerful women in India by Femina magazine and featured as one of the 200 most inspirational women from around the world in the book *Confessions to a Serial Womaniser–Secrets of the World's Inspirational Women*:

An incisive commentary on today's Indian society, this book blasts across all classes and gives the reader more than a peek into the reality that is life in our country today, and for the past several years. A must-read.

❧

Naina Balsaver Ahmed, former Miss India and famous singer:

An iconic beauty and one of my first friends in Delhi, Bindu Dalmia has been endowed with as much brain and emotion as the next intellectual! Any wonder this long-overdue book has a poetic licence to excite! Reading the initial excerpts has only left me wanting! Like the protagonist Akshraa, Bindu too has led a much-coveted life. Yet we know with ups come the leveller downs, to keep a check on reality.

Life's journey has only strengthened my charming friend of whom I am a strong critic and a silent supporter! May success shadow her.

Cheers!

~

Mona Verma, bestselling author of four books, including *God is a River* and *The White Shadow*:

Bindu Dalmia forays into the world of fiction with a brilliant start. *The Diary of a Lutyens' Princess* takes you through Akshraa's journey, fraught with her soul wanderings, her trysts and her battle within. The story has you hooked with its seamless narrative, the author's exemplary understanding of the socio-political climate and the profound sensitivity of a woman. A must-read for all, especially if you have known love and its underbelly, pain.

~

www.ingramcontent.com/pod-product-compliance
Lightning Source LLC
Chambersburg PA
CBHW060536310726
48982CB00009B/1279/J

9788129140395